GRIMDARK

Also available and coming soon from Black Hare Press

PUNK

GRIMDARK

WAR

Twitter: @BlackHarePress
Facebook: BlackHarePress
Website: www.BlackHarePress.com

First published in Australia in June 2022 by Black Hare Press

A catalogue record for this publication is available from the National Library of Australia

Cover design by Dawn Burdett
Editing by D. Kershaw
Formatting by Ben Thomas

Contents

I WORKED THE VERT

Darren Todd

The only reason anyone has even heard of the Vert is that the pathway is closed now. Or else you can bet—Freedom of Information Act or not—they never would have made any of this public.

You at least know the gist, I'm guessing: the only known portal to our mirror dimension was discovered in a small town in Kansas. *Like* our world. So similar you could shave looking at it, but different too. A vertical reflection of our reality. Or just the Vert. And right outside of Topeka. Centre of the US, which escaped exactly no one's notice.

Maybe things woulda turned out differently if the portal had cropped up in—I don't know—Switzerland. Maybe the Swiss would have...managed all of it a little better. But I can tell you, with all notions of patriotism aside, that if it had formed in, say, North Korea, things would have *also* been different, and worse than they turned out. I'd know. I might have been a low-level field operative, but for five years, from my first mission till the day things went to hell, I worked the Vert.

No matter what sort of theories have come out about how the Vert works, amateur-hour physicists talking about string theory, quantum mechanics, blah, blah blah, there's nothing our guys actually *in* the project—better paid and better equipped, let me assure you—didn't already figure out. And I had a pint with Dr Hopper himself probably a year after I'd started, and he explained it like this. Action/reaction: something happens here, the opposite happens there, not in the same way, not at the same time, but eventually, in "Vert-time" and however best puts things in balance. That's it. A school shooting on our side, a teacher inspires the next Nelson Mandela on their side. An earthquake over there means a verdant growing season over here.

That doesn't mean you can't tip the scales in your favour. This is where it gets interesting. 'Cause the worse things go for your mirror dimension, the better for you.

And when you disregard 24/7 news channels and social media, you might realise that times are pretty great for our side. Worldwide. Lower infant mortality rates, lower poverty rates, plummeting index crimes, higher wages and social equality. Across the board. Slowly, sure. And with pockets of regression. But as a whole? No doubt about it—better. You want to see real suffering, rewind a century; we've had a good run. Take a guess what that's meant for the last hundred years in the Vert.

So this caused a panic on our side; when was the balance coming? What would it look like? How can we maintain the advantage?

None of this came out during inter-dimensional talks, of course. To the Vert reps we hosted or the ones we met with on *that* side, we were all about balance. Every effort we made—every law and policy and police action—was only and ever about achieving equilibrium. Bringing them up to our standard of living while continuing to maintain that standard here.

But since chaos and suffering and disaster there mean better times here, why not go straight to the source? So, I and other operatives like me were tasked with tipping the scales—*keeping* the scales tipped—in our direction. That meant using the portal, going along as a rider to some delegate packet supposed to continue peace talks, and all that, breaking away, and then simulating random terrorist activity in the Vert. Specifically in the mirror dimension's version of the US. Gotta take care of home first, right?

That sounds terrible, I'm aware, but you gotta remember it was about balance. Working the Vert, violence does not beget violence. Say a heartland factory town has dried up. Jobs gone. Drugs and crime come in. Poverty, helplessness, decay. Sure, you can write your congressman about how off-shoring is hurting the working class and only benefiting a small minority of already wealthy people—the very ones funding that senator's reelection campaign, in fact. Yeah, good luck with that.

You go to that same spot in the Vert and find prosperity and abundance, even waste. You light a match in a place like that—some arson, a bombed building—maybe nobody even gets hurt, and you come home to find that a new tax policy has attracted a booming tech giant to open a branch or, at the very least, a real estate developer secures a grant to provide low-income housing. Whatever.

The more opulent a place, the greater the impact of discord. *That* is what I was fighting for. That was why I worked the Vert.

It was going fine till my last mission. Well, I didn't *know* it was my last mission. We didn't enter the Vert at the site of an op, of course. We routed everything through Topeka, so sometimes that meant several days of travel to reach an objective. There's no Delta flying the friendly skies in the Vert. So, it was tough to match up an op's location with where it was on our side.

Which was really disconcerting when I reached the village of Skalman. Reminded me a lot of a stint I pulled back in the Army in the Sudan. I'd seen real poverty, real hardship. Hand-to-mouth existence on *top* of dodging bullets and suffering oppression. That was Skalman. People beyond impoverished, beyond victimised. They barely had a breath left in them. All they had was a source of clean water. A well. Which, I found out, the Vert's version of the Peace Corps had dug for them a while back. And my job was to poison it.

I know what you're thinking: even if it *had* been an affluent area, what the hell was I doing poisoning a water supply? Not exactly setting off pipe bombs or staging a shooting. I thought the same thing. But as an operative, you roll with it. Take orders and then carry them out in your own way. But this had to be a mistake. Yeah, there was a well, and yeah, people were pulling fresh water from it, but this wasn't some flourishing city, no imbalance. At least, not on *their* side.

I had the payload in my hands, wasn't ten feet from the well, frozen with indecision. And this little girl came up to me, caked in mud, like she'd filled her wheelbarrow with earth using only her fingers. Face sunken, eyes unfocused. She saw me, and she held out her hands, cupped, like—what?—like I'd give her a Hershey bar or something. I was clean, dry, clothes unmarred by whatever horrors this village had suffered for God knows how long. She looked at the payload, wrapped in a water-soluble oil cloth. Reached out for it.

"No," I told her and shook my head. "It's bad. It's... poison."

She didn't understand, of course. But must have read in my body language that I couldn't help her. She didn't cry or even keep trying; she just turned and walked away, the bottoms of her feet like the pad of a dog's paw.

So I came back, mission failed. But not before exhausting my skills at land nav and celestial navigation to figure out where I was over there. I immediately resigned my field operative status, seemingly out of shame for—as I put it—losing the payload during a scuffle with a local criminal element. Believable, given the landscape.

I took a job riding a desk, fetching coffee for operative handlers, pretty much. A step down is being nice, but I figured I might still keep an eye on things, even give a nudge here and there. Turns out there was no need. A month into that job and the portal closed for good. Word was a bomb on *their* side. Can't say I blame them.

We were reassigned the next morning after signing a book's worth of nondisclosure agreements. I just resigned altogether, and after my screw up in Skalman, no one tried to stop me.

So what did I find? On this side, at the same site as pitiful little Skalman? It was a golf course not far outside DC. US DoD property, technically attached to an army base, but mostly a vacay spot for visiting dignitaries, military brass, politicians. I made a trip over there, fortunately still with enough credentialism to get on base. Found a groundskeeper, or he found me. I stood there, open-mouthed, staring, picturing that very spot in the Vert. I could see the dirt, the ash, that girl with the dog-pad feet.

"Can I help you, sir?" the groundskeeper asked me.

"Anything wrong with this place?" I said.

"Not sure I follow, sir?"

"I heard you were having problems, or something to that effect."

The guy—a lieutenant, sharp uniform—looked out across the rolling greens. "You must be the lawn expert the greens committee was bringing in."

"Exactly that," I told him. "So, what's going on here?"

"Look at the colouration," he said and waved a hand

out to the links. The greens had a tan patch here and there, but otherwise looked like any golf course I'd ever been to. "Costs a fortune to keep it up."

"Hard water?" I guessed.

"Shit, if only. The water ain't the problem. Never should have laid down Bermuda in this climate to begin with. Drought tolerant, sure, but more than a single cold snap, and it gets pissy."

I shrugged. "I wasn't going to say anything...."

"Then you know it's true. Every frost we get is a kick in the teeth." He bent down and pinched a few blades, held them up, searching them and obviously seeing something I couldn't, before throwing them in seeming disgust to the breeze. "You got any ideas?"

Oh, I had ideas. Looking out at the rolling hills, seeing the early birds schmoozing, deciding the fate of underling grunts and agents alike while indulging in the safest competition imaginable. And this while that little girl in Skalman woke every morning to an empty belly, where she had to ignore the laundry list of ailments no doubt riddling her system just to keep that broken machine she called a body moving. Hell, the poison might have been a blessing, but not when the only thing at stake was greener fucking pastures for the foreign dignitaries and politicians who haunted this course.

"Lemme take a look at your irrigation systems," I said.

As if descending into a bunker, the lieutenant led me down into the beating heart of the golf course: the irrigation and fertilisation machine-works. At some level, all systems work the same. If it's big and loud, it's important. I'd memorised every hazmat symbol, ours and the Vert's, so whether it was turning something up or turning something off, fucking things up wasn't rocket science. Given the right access, an angry chimp could have done my job.

"The rainwater reclaimer helps," the lieutenant said. "A little. I doubt it pays for itself, but it at least lets us apply two different additives. One in the vat and another via the fertiliser feed, since the sprinklers pull from the reservoir before tapping into the water main. You try to take a drink from a water fountain around here on a hot day when we've been watering all night, you're going to look like a first grader."

"Tell me you've tried altering the PH," I said. What I knew about the science of liquids could almost fill a glass of water, but I said this with an accusation behind it. This guy had messed up. Those tan patches garnering part snickers, part derision from the fat cats—they were on him.

"Well, I…" he trailed off.

I sighed, as if barely able to hide my disgust, as if this was a huge waste of my talent. "Grab me some soil samples from each hole. I'm gonna fetch my testing kit and tackle things in here. With a little luck, we might find our tipping point sometime today. You got the keys?" I held out my hand, palm up, fingers jiggling with an impatient gimme gesture.

The lieutenant touched the ring of keys at his waist protectively. "I'll just leave the hatch unlocked if that's all right. I'll need the keyring for—"

"Yeah, that'll work. We'll touch base back here, what, two o'clock? You be done by then?"

He looked to the concrete floor, perhaps spinning his mental reel of the task at hand, the pain in the ass of core sampling eighteen holes. "Yeah, that'll work," he said, echoing my verbiage—something people do when they feel inferior.

"We'll fix this," I said, supplanting his uncertainty with confidence.

I drove to the BX for the two ingredients I needed to right the balance, either of which would likely find that lieutenant standing tall before the man tomorrow morning. But he would recover. The golf course wouldn't.

First, I dumped blue pond colourant into the rainwater reclaimer. The stuff stank like the concentrated shit that gave linoleum floors their shine. Likely the brass looking to talk shop over a few holes wouldn't find the result quite so aesthetically pleasing. No matter, since step two meant pouring glyphosate into the fertiliser injection system. Nothing like a little weed killer for a swan song.

I felt bad for the lieutenant but hoped ruining that golf course meant the girl got a pair of shoes. Raised a goat. Planted a few seeds that bore fruit. Stuff would get better for her, and no worse for wear here. Not really.

But I started thinking. If balance is inevitable, then messing with the scales is folly to begin with. Who knows? Too many fat years for us and lean years for the Vert and maybe Mother Nature will decide to open up one of those super volcanoes lying dormant. Or maybe some missileer will figure it's time to lob a nuke at Moscow, just because it feels like the right thing to do.

The scumbags here who ordered me to kill innocent civilians so they could golf on greener pastures wouldn't give a rat's ass if their decadence cost millions of lives when the balance came due, I have no doubt of that. I also have no doubt that right now—this very second—there are rooms full of brilliant men and women looking for any way to reopen the portal.

Maybe this time the Vert will be waiting, and it'll be our turn to suffer for their enjoyment.

A SIREN'S DILEMMA

Nathan Slemp

As your breath makes such beautiful bubbles, I wonder if I should stop.

You're all so pretty below the waves. Everything is. But you can't survive here, can you? You scream and drown, and the sharks carry you away.

But what else can I do? Go to the Queen Below and ask her to return my humanity? Turn my tentacles back into legs, my scales into skin, and try to find a nice man? Because that worked out so well last time?

Of course, you can't answer any more.

Maybe I should ask the next man *before* dragging him under.

GRIMDAR

R.S. Nevil

What sort of hell was this?

What sort of desolate world had they sent him to?

The wind whipped around him. Greyish dust caught within its grasp. The ground was covered in it.

In the distance, he could see plumes of smoke drifting into the horizon, the setting sun framing the outline of destruction. Red waters filled the nearby lakes and streams, giving off the impression of blood.

He had heard stories of this place. It was a place where people went to die. A place so horrible that even the wicked feared it.

It was Grimdar.

The prison world.

ATTRITION

Liam Hogan

They fought their battles on endless rocky plains. No soil beneath which to bury their dead, no wood for funeral pyres. They incorporated them into their defences: walls that grew taller with every pointless battle, barricades that sprouted arrow shafts until the archers harvested them. Ladders of broken spears and shattered swords, the trenches between, slick with blood and gore, overrun by rats, flies, and disease.

The war consumed the best of every generation.

Fifty years. A hundred, it had been going. Two hundred.

Something *stirred.*

Something that found the mounds of corpses fertile ground.

Something was hungry…for more.

SOLDIER OF FORTUNE

Maggie D. Brace

Clinging tenaciously to her leg, the filthy child stirred something long forgotten—an emotion she hadn't felt in many years. Staring down at the enormous pleading eyes, she sheathed her sword and, in one deft movement, swung the mewling creature up and onto her back. Striding forwards, she continued her search for enemy survivors to dispatch. The child gripped her neck tighter and whispered in her ear, "Thank you." Suddenly, it all came back to her, why she had buried that queasy feeling of compassion in the first place. Peeling the child off her back, she soldiered wearily onwards, alone.

FOR UNCONDITIONAL LOVE

Michelle Chermaine Ramos

I stroked Nyx's lifeless body on the altar, his still black fur cast with an amber glow from the candlelight. He was my most trusted companion. Cats don't lie, they don't cheat, they don't stab you in the back. No human gives unconditional love like that.

The grimoire said the spell would bring the dead back to life but required a sacrifice of one heart for another lifetime—or two to make him immortal.

I turned and walked towards my former lover and my best friend; eyes wide, gagged, bound, and trembling on the floor. Nyx never liked them anyway.

Piñatas

Mike Murphy

The policewoman found the piñata, the one the weird killer admitted using to hold the mementos of his murders: a hand, an ear…whatever pleased him. Here—finally!—was the evidence needed for conviction.

At the station, as the officer cut into the unicorn-shaped thing, it *cracked.* A bloody, foul-smelling pool of anatomy sluiced from the party favour and onto the table. She resisted the urge to vomit, which grew stronger as the mass stood upon a child's foot and, mouthless, cried pitifully to be put out of the conjoined misery the killer had made of his trophies.

BLACKTOOTH

Barend Nieuwstraten III

Cold waves of the southern sea crashed against the wooden hull of his longboat as Svuld rummaged through the nearest sack of looted foreign treasures. He peered inside at the spoils of another raid as his men rowed to the pounding drum. They proudly bragged of their recent exploits to the very men who fought beside them as they laboured to move their vessel. None were disinterested in hearing the stories again and again. For they would repeat their tales to perfect the art of telling them until the small fleet of boats once more scraped upon the shores of Froskheim, where eager ears awaited. Tales to be told over horns of mead, of the brave raid upon the green shores of Westmeer, where men who once wiped out the orcs of those lands failed to protect their treasures from Svuld's party of reavers.

Though he looked forward to spilling sacks of gold at

his jarl's feet, Svuld desired to bury his hands in the captured jewels, gems, goldcraft, and sculptures of which they had relieved the Westmeerians. He ran his fingers over the white stone of the object that claimed his interest above all others. He had never felt anything quite so smooth. A skull so large, if it had been made of bone, the man it belonged to would have to have been at least ten feet tall. Deep within its sockets, there were great rubies for eyes and tears of gold that ran down its cheekbones towards its obsidian teeth. He couldn't wait to poke his knife inside and pluck out the precious gems, though he dared not do it now lest he launch one out over the bow and into the sea by accident. He did not make his attack on the green land to make such an offering to the gods of the sea.

He turned the great skull in the sack upon feeling a hole in the back of it. When he looked, there were five; four down the right side and one wider on the left. He held his fingers out and pulled his hand closer to his eye to make it seem bigger compared to the object. No mistake. They were finger holes, but for a hand twice the size of his own. *Who made this thing?* he wondered. For its size, he should not have been able to lift it. Not that it was convenient to do so, but it was not simply carved from solid stone. It was hollow inside by the feel of it, skilfully crafted through means Svuld could not imagine.

"Does your sad friend with the pretty eyes have a name?" Olgrette asked, watching him marvel and fondle at the treasure from the northern land of green shores.

"Blacktooth," Svuld said, smiling at her. "I think he should be called Blacktooth."

* * *

A storm soon came that carried them from their path. A great white mist filled the air and swallowed the sun, as all directions became as one. They lost count of every turn the angry waves forced upon them, compelling them hither and thither into the unfamiliar. Of the six ships that left home, only four left the shores of the northland when the Westmeerian's retribution had come down upon them for their bountiful raid. Only three ships Svuld could see now, and one was that upon which he now stood.

A great shadow flew overhead, drawing all faces upwards as it swooped past, dragging a harsh cold draft in its wake. With their heads upturned, they were unprepared when a great collision jolted them, knocking those standing off their feet. Svuld tumbled into his oarmen as others were tossed about violently. The timber of Svuld and Bjenmr's longboats protested as the two vessels met, scraping as they pushed against one another. Oars, not raised in time, broke, crushed between the two vessels, flicking splintered shards of wood everywhere as they loudly snapped. All wrestled to recompose themselves quickly, but the source of their distraction still held primary concern. All eyes soon turned back to the foggy sky.

The shadow moved above them, sounding like the deep cracking of wet sails flicking in the wind. A great screeching roar filled the sky and echoed across the water as a flying beast passed them in favour of another of their small fleet. There was a hissing spray, but not of crashing briny foam. It sounded cold, somehow frostier than ice or snow. Then there was the sound of men screaming in a way no warrior should, followed by the yelling and banging of paired axes the way raiders did to taunt their foes. It put fire in Svuld's heart amidst the cold storm until he heard again the crack of wood and splintering. Too deep to be oars. It was the sound of a breaking mast, followed by men, weapons, and sacks stuffed with gold, plunging into the sea. Gargled cries of drowning men in the coldest waters were silenced by another piercing spray.

"Frostdrakes," Bjenmr called to his crew and friends as the drums returned, called upon by their captains at a hastened pace.

* * *

Upon some stony coast, two ships crashed and broke, but enough wood for three washed ashore. A cold wind howled and chilled the brine that was soaked into their furs, hair, and worn skins, turning the frost even colder against their flesh. The men ran beyond the grey rocks and sands to the white covered land, carrying sacks of coin and goldcraft from the green kingdom in the north.

A shadow grew again as the flapping of large wings haunted the misty sky above. The white scaled beast descended, staying its wings to glide past, and blasted its breath of frost against a dozen men who fell, frozen to the beach before they could draw their axes. The wet sand turned white, as crystals of long-frost formed in its wake. The white crystals that sprouted when frostdrake breath hit wet surfaces was a lasting mark of the beast known by all in the colder kingdoms.

Other men in its path hurled rocks and threw blades at the beast as it swooped low towards them. It turned and twisted, knocking men down with its head of backward curving horns, thwarting their assault. It took one man in its jaws before flapping its great wings to lift itself and took another pair in its talons. It rose into the sky, returning two men from far above, their bodies breaking on the rocks before the arms and legs of another landed on the icy sand, spilling blood that steamed upon the cold beach.

Spotting caves in the rocky hills, Bjenmr and Svuld led their men to the only shelter they could hope to reach, half a mile from where they crashed ashore. Their number grew few as they ran the distance, picked away by the great beast. They ducked and weaved as they attempted to close the gap, using the growing number of larger rocks to evade the attacks. As they huddled in the mouth of the cave, they looked back to see the creature, joined by another, devouring their fallen brothers and sisters. Tearing apart those who had survived the first assault but were too broken to flee to the caves. Some managed to crawl away, dragging their wounded bodies along sand and rock as the beasts gorged themselves on a feast of frozen and savaged men and women. When Bjenmr and Svuld were satisfied that the frostdrakes were too busy eating to pay them mind, they snuck out and pulled who they could back to the caves. Gathering all they could, they explored their newfound shelter, too narrow for the beasts to follow, where they would likely need to hide for days.

Surrounded by dark grey stone and ice, those who could wield weapons held them ready as they wandered deeper inside the rocky hills. Strands of dull light shone down from cracks in the high rocky ceiling above, periodically illuminating the path ahead through incomplete cover. Bjenmr found an old log pile half covered by ice, and a firepit made by men now frozen dead, scattered throughout the cave, half trapped in ice themselves and preserved by the cold. The flesh of the dead, blackened by frostbite, supplemented the motivation of their own cold skin in hastening their attempts to start a fire. Once lit, the remaining few huddled closely around it, drying their garments and resting for a day.

As Olgrette and Bjenmr counted the remaining gold that made it with them, Svuld dug his knife into Blacktooth's eyes to pluck from the sockets the great rubies within. Breaking the tip off his short blade in the attempt, Svuld pressed on, determined. He would not be dissuaded from his task. Committed to separating the gems from the stubborn giant skull, he continued to tamper with it, using his pointless dagger, but never managing to budge them in his fruitless endeavour.

* * *

Hunger and impatience stirred for days as their

number waned, even in hiding. Some were claimed by the cold, despite the fire that melted much of the ice that preserved the corpses of those who came before them. Others succumbed to wounds inflicted by the creatures that saw them cornered so. Svuld wondered how long it would be before they too would join the frozen dead to serve as a warning to future souls who might take refuge in this bitter place. He looked at the decayed faces of the cave's earlier inhabitants and wondered if they too had been forced ashore and came to this place to shelter from the white-scaled predators.

"How long have you been here?" he asked them. "Where did you come from and where were you hoping to go? Did death come gently in the night, or did hunger grow until that's all you were? Devoured by the aching need for sustenance?"

Olgrette pulled him away and back to the fire. "They have earned their rest," she said. "Let them have it in peace."

Svuld placed Blacktooth on a rocky shelf at the end of the cave. He positioned it so that it was watching over them all, and he stopped accosting it when his blade had chipped too many times. He sat in quiet despair, robbed of the two vices that distracted him.

There were some who didn't sleep, claiming Blacktooth called to them in the night, inviting them to close their eyes and sleep forever. Others swore they heard the great skull whispering as they slept, conspiring with the dead, inviting them to wake. Some even claimed that the blackened dead they shared the cave with had moved in the night, shifting where they lay by each dawn.

Olgrette told them they were merely going mad with hunger and need only last a little longer. Just until the frostdrakes, who slept on the beach nearby, left in search of fresh prey. With all they had eaten of their friends, it was a feast of days they had prepared upon the beach. Svuld began to realise that no one had actually checked the beach in days. All loath to leave the fire, and rendered tired by their empty bellies.

It wasn't until those rotted, frozen dead of the cave, old and new, blackened and blue, began to stir and rise, that the survivors finally knew it had not been madness in their ears in the night. Blacktooth had enlisted the long-forgotten dead and roused them from their mortal slumber. The raiders made their stand at first, fighting the dead who made as many in their stead, thinning the raider's numbers even further. Indefatigable, the skinny, dark corpses gave a relentless assault, not cold, nor hungry, nor weakened or afflicted by injury. They could not be deterred.

The fierceness of the fight seemed to diminish the further the raiders were pushed back from Svuld's treasured sculpture. The dead seemed to be herding the living towards the entrance of the cave as Blacktooth's frozen followers deterred reapproach, rather than pursue. It seemed they were protecting the great stone skull from the raiders as they evicted them from their shelter.

Beyond their dwindled number and the impossibility of retaliation, the four that survived agreed that Blacktooth should stay behind, cursed and forgotten, surrounded by his own kind. He watched the Froskheim raiders leave his new cave home with his red ruby eyes and golden tears.

* * *

In the absence of the frostdrakes, who by now were either stalking the sea once more or perhaps still sleeping off the meal of their companions somewhere else, the raiders searched the coast until they found a boat to steal. They took again to the sea, now mercifully calmer and they thanked the gods for seeing them home when they eventually found their way back to their own land with their two remaining sacks of gold.

With only four of them left from their small fleet, they returned to newly made widows, orphans, and the old who had lost their sons and daughters. An army of brave raiders lost for a treasure, mostly sitting somewhere at the bottom of the sea, or abandoned in a cave to which none would dare tread again.

They told their hero's story of their brave raid which brought some comfort to the many who had lost, but then spoke of the dark tidings that followed. A great tale, amended by disaster. They warned their tribe, "Beware the great skull with ruby eyes. Blacktooth cries gold and, if you claim him, so will you."

The Dark Eye

Barend Nieuwstraten III

Ered lay dying on the battlefield staring at the sun, changed by a blanket of burning woodland's smoke. No longer a brilliant disc of blinding brightness, but an orb of dark writhing slag, staring back at him like a great demon's eye in the sky.

"The dark sun sees us all," he yelled, drawing close an enemy hewing his fallen comrades where they lay. As a pilum impaled his belly, he opened a thigh with a dagger. His enemy collapsed beside him, leaking vital fluid. Ered turned his enemy's face towards the sky. "See the sun's true face this day."

THE SILVER COG

William Bartlett

My father invented the cog hammer. A simple, two-handed blunt weapon with a massive cog that spun from the charge of a thousand arcing volts. No one cared until he stepped into the arena and decorated it with someone's blood. It was the first and final place he was given the respect he deserved. There, on the oily sanded arena floor, he truly lived. In this world, violence is power. Strength is currency.

There was no doctor at the time to tend to the victims of the junker arena. Nor were there tools necessary to safely amputate the rot in my father's leg, that spread to his heart. His only possession when he died was a silver cog, small enough to wear on a silver chain around his neck, but large enough to represent his greatest invention. It would have been lost to his killer, had he died on the arena floor.

I dedicated my life to medicine, so I could save lives

instead of taking them. I was seen as weak. Scum. But my ideals spread throughout Junk City, the third largest megacity on this continent. And the arena saw fewer numbers over the years, but was never fully forsaken.

I lectured fighters as I healed them. Some found new lifestyles, some died, and some ignored me entirely. I found love, and we brought a boy into the world. I raised my boy to grow into a man like me. But by the time he did, he had suffered a bit too much ridicule from peers. He developed a fear of turning out like me, though I found comfort in his respect for my choices. But when he experienced his first heartbreak, the rage influenced his choice to follow his grandfather's path instead.

When my son was old enough to be recruited as a fighter in the arena, he was. After much ignored pleading, I was left with a difficult choice; accept *his* choice, or become his enemy. So, I gave him the silver cog for luck—small enough to wear on a silver chain around his neck, but large enough to represent his grandfather's greatest invention.

But now I am here, trembling amid the most powerful dilemma of my life. You see, I *chose* the life of medicine and of humility. I *chose* to be bound by honour and oath. I *chose* to save lives, regardless of whether they be friend or foe. But I am still a product of this violent world, and a child of turmoil. I suffer the same homicidal tendencies as the arena fighters.

Like *them*, I battle. I battle with the decision to amputate the leg of the man before me, like I have always wished I could have done for my father. But if I do, I will save the life of this evil enemy. For he wears a silver cog—small enough to wear on a silver chain around his neck, but large enough to represent his victory over my son.

SACRIFICIAL LAMB

Vijayaraj Mahendraraj

"You know, people forget where advancements originate. They shun engineers of the machinery whilst they are cogs themselves. The big picture. That's what you're a part of," he said, donning the grimy black gloves. The muffled voice was strained.

"Now, now. Don't fret. Just think about it this way. You are amongst many unselfish souls that will save us all. A sacrificial lamb to appease the deities and I am simply tasked to uphold their will." He raised the dulled scalpel.

"Every vitreous, a virtue. Every bit of bile, a smile. Every exsanguination, a salvation. Ah, where shall we begin?"

ORGANIC WINE

Ryan Tan

I spread Manuka honey on the inside of his cheeks. Lemongrass paste on the roof of his mouth. I lifted his chin and poured six glasses of Concord grape juice down his throat. Violet streams escaped his lips, mingling with the blood from his forehead. Twenty-four hours later, I wheeled in a keg and removed the lid. Starting with the strap around his throat, I released him. He slumped forward, sloshing black liquid into the keg. I filled a cocktail glass and sniffed. Oak, death, fermented grapes. The bitter brew seared my throat. Nothing like a glass of organic wine.

BATTLE SPOILS

Stephen Sottong

"Don't disturb us," Stilgarn yelled down to his men as he mounted the tower stairs by twos and forced the maiden's chamber door. She lay on her bed in diaphanous robes, revealing more than concealing. He slammed the door, tossing his sword aside. "I've got something for you," he roared, opening the crotch of his armour.

"Just what I was looking for," she said, plucking the knife hidden beneath her and jamming it into the gap in his armour.

Her mock-screams covered his. The eyehole provided access for the coup-de-grâce. Then she stole his armour, concealing her ride to freedom.

THE SHADOW'S PATTERN

Chad A.B. Wilson

Novices milled about, readying bodies for burial. Ten hells, it smelled, even with the doors open.

"I'm looking for Berean," Brock told a woman of about forty.

She wiped her hands, nodding.

"I'm Brock, Guardian of Falsea."

"Ah, the famous commander. I understand you've been responsible for many of the Sheath's acquisitions over the years."

Brock shrugged. "I saved as many as I took, I hope."

"An awful calculus, isn't it?" she said. "Sacrificing to save."

"Greater good, and all that."

"I assume you're here because of the organless female?"

He was actually there because of her uncle, Lord Jerune. He hadn't met the lord until that morning when the man had stormed into Brock's palace office. He was like many lords—entitled, overbearing, and expecting obsequiousness. He yelled, stomped, and called Brock a "good-for-nothing bureaucrat." Said he'd have Brock's job if the commander didn't find his niece's killer. Brock calmed him with a glass of whiskey, and the man turned from an irate lord into a frightened child. The man had seen the girl's corpse, and what he'd seen disturbed him.

That tension was familiar to Brock—he avoided death, yet he sought it, too. His relationship with the Sheath was complicated.

Berean reached out for Brock's hand, and he looked up at her. "We all need a guide," she said. Brock shrugged and took her hand. The contact was odd—wrong, almost—like a mother leading a wayward child. She parted two curtains and ushered Brock inside. "We separated her, of course." Berean moved to the only table with what was unmistakably a body hidden under a sheet. "The ones who saw her had to be relieved of their duties for the day. Maybe for the week. Maybe forever. The Sheath's work is not always pretty."

"I'm aware."

Berean removed the covering, and Brock took a deep breath.

"She wasn't the first, you know."

* * *

Brock's walk up the steps was more difficult than usual. He'd seen a lot of death. Sheath take him, he'd caused a lot of death, men and monsters both.

"We shut her eyes, but we couldn't close her jaw," Berean had told him. "Someone reached in through her mouth and removed her organs one by one. Her chest and abdomen are practically empty." She motioned as she said it, reaching in again and again. Brock winced. "The mouth was forced open so wide, the jaw broke and the oesophagus deformed. Looks almost like she's still screaming, doesn't it? She was alive while it happened. At least for the first part."

Brock shook his head and continued up the stairs. What was a gods damn lord doing working in Sheathenside, anyway? Lords and ladies didn't have occupations, as far as Brock could tell—unless telling people what to do and making Brock's life miserable was a job. If Wyvaren was really a lord, he was an unusual one.

A large room opened up, its roof propped up by columns. Rows of closed, ceiling-high cabinets stood in the centre. A ladder would be needed to get to the top, at least ten feet above him. Papers stacked neatly in piles covered a table at the entry. Several well-placed lamps illuminated most of the cavernous room.

"Yes?" a voice boomed.

Brock looked around. "Lord Wyvaren?"

A skinny old man with short-cropped white hair

stepped from between two cabinets. "Who are you?"

"I'm Commander Brock. Berean told me to speak to you."

"Well, you are."

Brock blinked.

"What do you want, Commander?"

"Berean told me there were other bodies with missing organs."

"Happens all the time." The man walked off.

Brock followed. "With organs pulled out through their mouths."

"That's a different story. Precision matters."

Brock sighed. *Lords.*

They turned through more rows of cabinets and exited the stacks to the south wall which was covered—floor to ceiling—with maps. To be precise, all copies of the same map—Falsea. Brock stopped to examine one. Small nails dotted the capital city.

"The Sheath doesn't stop his work for you."

Brock sighed. *Gods damn lords.*

"Special map, just for them," Wyvaren said, gesturing to an identical map. There were nails all over the place, each with a note beneath.

Brock shook his head. "What am I looking at?"

"Falsea."

"I get that. What are the nails?"

"Sites of murders like the one you described."

"What? Why am I just now hearing about this? There's got to be at least a hundred nails!"

"Ninety-eight, to be precise."

"When was the first?"

Wyvaren grabbed a lantern off a table and held it closer before pointing to one. "In 528."

"Five hundred years ago?"

"Four hundred and thirty-seven, to be precise."

"Ten hells, old man, you mean these are all the bodies in your records?"

"Don't call me old. And no, these are only the records of bodies with organs removed through their mouths. That's what you asked about, is it not?"

"So, this has happened before?"

"Ninety-eight times since 528, to be precise. As the scriptures tell us, 'The moon and the Sheath are one. They have each seen the world anew through time and time and time. Its rebirth every evening returns each night the same.'"

Brock squinted. "Do you see a pattern?"

Wyvaren turned to Brock, then back to the map, then let out a hearty guffaw.

Brock sighed.

Finally, Wyvaren recovered. "I'm sorry, Commander, but that's gods damn funny." He laughed again.

"And precisely why is that funny?"

The man gestured to the entire wall of maps. "Why do you think I'm here? What do you think these maps represent?"

"Death?"

Wyvaren shook his head. "Patterns."

* * *

Brock stood in the alley, watching the street, a member of the City Watch beside him. The rain sprinkled down, the sky dark, lanterns on the sides of the buildings flickering in the wind. Brock pulled his cloak tighter. The temperature had dropped. He hated cold and rain together. He brought out his flask and pulled from it, then turned to the woman beside him.

She looked at it, then up at Brock, questioningly. Brock shrugged. She took the flask, pulled, and handed it back.

"Thanks, Commander."

"Ten hells, you're stuck here with me. Has to be something good about it, right?"

"So, you think the killer's going to come by here?"

"No idea, Peresh. But we have these blocks surrounded. If it's out there, we'll see it. Light your lamp, soldier. Rain's about to come down." Peresh was a good kid. Been with the Watch a few months after a stint in the King's Finest. Brock figured she'd make it to colonel one day.

"Commander!"

Brock jogged to the soldier running toward them.

"Someone saw it?"

"Yes, Commander! They're following it." He stopped to catch his breath.

Brock pushed him. "Lead the way!"

They ran, Peresh just behind Brock. Another member

of the Watch met them and ran alongside. "They're still following it, Commander," he said. "The thing's fast!"

"Thing?" Peresh said.

"It isn't human, whatever it is!"

Two members of the Watch stood in the street, panting. They saluted. "Commander!"

"Is it in there?" Brock asked.

"It slipped right in, squeezed between the doorframe."

Brock looked up at the five-story building, full of small low-rent tenements, with similar buildings crammed all over the poorer district of Hemis One. "Go find another patrol and bring them back. Peresh, on me. Quen, you and the others search the first and second. We'll search the third and fourth. Meet on the fifth."

"Yes, sir!"

Brock opened the door and took to the stairs. A lamp burned low in the stairwell.

"Peresh, get the lamp ready," he called back to her.

They hit the landing of the third floor and stopped. Halls branched in two directions, both dark. Brock looked, then pulled his sword from the scabbard that hung on his belt. He smiled at the *zing!* it made when he unleashed it. The Sheath wanted its acquisitions.

"Need that lamp, Peresh."

"Almost, sir..."

They walked nearly to the end of the hall. Then Brock turned and ran back to the other branch. Peresh came up behind him, the lamp burning brightly. At the end, Brock turned and ran back to the stairs.

Brock took the steps two at a time, then chose the right hall at random. He caught a glimpse of something ahead, like a shadow gliding. He ran forwards, and it turned, the blackness of it filling the hallway, facing him. Then it turned and slid inside.

"Ten hells," Peresh muttered.

Brock ran to the door—locked. He stood back, braced himself, and kicked the door inward before rushing in. A lamp illuminated a one-room tenement. A motionless man, with eyes closed, sat at a desk with a plate in front of him, vials scattered around.

Something knocked into Brock, and he stumbled forwards, barely catching himself. Peresh pulled out her blade, but she was pushed forwards. The lamp flew, smashing beside the bed. The oil ignited. Flames licked up the bedding.

Peresh lay on the ground, scrambling to get herself upright. Brock saw the creature then—a man cloaked in shadow. He sliced at it, but it slid out of the sword's way, as if it were so thin, the sword couldn't catch it. He tried a horizontal swing, then another, pushing it back through the room. It hit the wall, then danced around to the side, but Brock's blade caught it. Bits of shadow flaked off, like it was made of a black liquid, bubbles coming apart when he struck it.

It knocked into Brock, but Peresh was there, and she sliced into it, parts of the thing sloughing off in black droplets that floated in the air. Brock came at it from behind, but it ducked down and slid out of the way, floating to the top of the bed, which blazed around it. The shadow hovered, the flames licking around its strange corporeal form. It manoeuvred between the individual tongues of fire.

Peresh and Brock both swiped at it. Black droplets sizzled as they hit the flames. More bits of shadow rained down and dissipated in the fire as Peresh slashed it again.

The shadow leaped forward, pushing into Peresh, carrying her across the room. She slammed into the window, which shattered behind her. Brock ran and sliced through it again, but it turned and pushed. Brock stumbled against the bed into the flames, his sword clanging to the floor as he rolled off, clambering out of the fire. He flailed frantically to put out the fire licking up his arm.

Brock knelt and checked himself. The shadow loomed above Peresh, who stood motionless as the thing held her jaw and reached into her open mouth. She watched with wide eyes as the hand slid into her throat.

Brock ran forward and grabbed the shadow monster, surprised by its fleshiness. He grunted and flung it toward the window. Shattered glass and shadow burst through the window into the darkness and rain, which swept into the room.

The shadow's limb reached wildly as it fell and caught onto Peresh, who yelped as it latched onto her and dragged her out into the darkness with it.

"Ten hells," Brock muttered as he lunged.

He caught her hand. She dangled out the window, not even bothering to scream, her hair flowing in the rain, her terrified eyes staring up at him. The shadow was gone, as if washed away by the rain.

Lanterns dotted the city that spread out beneath Peresh.

"Don't look down," Brock said.

She looked back, even more terror in her eyes, her mouth moving. She kicked into the side of the tenement, her other hand flailing, knocking into Brock's hand, the only thing keeping her from falling four stories to the cobbled alley.

"Stop...jerking," Brock strained against her, tried to use his leverage on the windowsill to pull her up and not slip out the window with her.

Peresh looked up at him again. "Please," she whispered, her voice raspy.

Brock pulled, but the glass cut him, and he let go of the sill momentarily. She jerked, but Brock held tight. He found another hold and pulled.

He ignored the wave of heat from behind him.

The wind caught her. Her legs swayed. She screamed, reaching for him.

"Stop," Brock said, straining. She was almost to the window ledge now. Brock braced his foot against the window. Almost.

He felt the wind, the rain coming down in sheets that blasted through the shattered window. She jerked again. Her fingers tore at his hand, pulling them. "Stop!" Brock yelled, but it was too late. She slipped.

Brock fell back. "Gods damn it!" He leaped back to

the window. He heard the thud before he saw her lying there in the alley, blood just beginning to pool beneath her head, the rain streaming down. He sighed and felt the fury rise, a heat within him. The Sheath would have more acquisitions today.

He turned to the man sitting at the desk. By all appearances, he had not moved a muscle. But something burned on the plate in front of him, and the man breathed it in.

Theurgy. Most called it magic. Consume a part of someone, and the theurgist could use that person's magical potential to effect change in the world. Like creating shadow monsters. He felt the chill on the back of his neck and shivered. That always happened when someone used magic. Like the atmosphere was charged with it.

He turned and another shadow creature stood before him.

"Sheath take me," he muttered. He grabbed his sword from the ground and turned to the man at the desk. Muttering "Sometimes there's nothing to be done," he slipped the blade through his skull. The man jerked, then slumped. His head slid off the blade and thumped to the table. Brock turned back to the shadow monster, which fell into a million black droplets. "Should have done that in the first place."

Quen and the others rushed in, swords drawn. The flames now burned across half the room.

"Wake up the tenement," he told them. "Get a water brigade going."

They sprang into action.

* * *

"Lord Wyvaren!" Brock called.

The old man's face appeared amid the cabinets. "Ah, Commander. You found your organ collector, I assume."

"That, we did."

"A theurgist, consuming organs to work his magic?"

Brock's mouth dropped. "No one else seems to believe in such."

They walked to a table, and the old man brought over a bottle and two glasses. He poured two fingers each.

"You can't see the patterns I've seen and not believe the Sheath weaves them all."

Brock nodded and drank. "I need you to track these things, Wyvaren."

"I already do, Commander. Yet no one bothers to ask."

"Well, I'm asking. You see patterns, I want to know about it."

Wyvaren smiled. "I see them everywhere."

THE SHORES OF TRIPLE E

John H. Dromey

Searching for signs of life on an alien planet, a company of marines discovered an extra-large set of humanoid footprints on a sandy beach.

"Wouldn't it be something if a Sasquatch or two somehow managed to travel here ahead of us?" Sergeant Blair mused. "A mating pair perhaps? They could have established a small population by now."

Before he could respond, Captain Schuster received a disturbing report from the company's radio operator.

"Bad news, sir. Our basecamp was overrun by hordes of huge hairy creatures. No survivors."

"Apparently, Sergeant Blair got it wrong. The *limited* bigfoot population is on Earth."

Hear Them

J.D. Wolff

They walk with the night.

They're silent, but the wind softly rasping against the rusting iron of their armour distinguishes them from the rustling three. Also, they walk. Their old leather boots squish with each step, like they're slippery with blood.

It's a sound that can't be mistaken.

They were kings. They dressed in gold and purple. Their heads carried the weight of crowns and power.

They were warriors. They fought battles. The steel of their swords was sharp and shone with blood and glory.

Now, they're forgotten. They're stories.

But hear them.

They walk with the night. The dead.

THE HAND OF JUSTICE

Gray W. Wolfe

Evil manifests itself in many ways. It is a festering cancer, growing to a bloody bulbous proportion. In the Black Lands, where daemon, monsters, and those accursed wolves, the Blymarch, infest in equal abundance, I must be vigilant. I must be the Hand of Justice, for I am the *Crea'dynl*, the sanctified Inquisitor, ordained by the Empress, the Obsidian Goddess, herself!

This night felt different, the stars twinkling, casting their wretched gaze upon this city of sin and offal below.

"Soffwyll na'Lluedd is out this night," I said to myself in a grumbling whisper, sword in hand as I stalked my prey through the streets of Soer Dawn. Soffwyll na'Lleudd—the Insanity Moon. I couldn't see it, but I certainly felt its presence, its whispers imparting secrets to me no sane man could fathom, let alone retain such heretical knowledge.

There. I found the house serving as the lair of an abomination, one who possesses the skin of a man, but beats the heartbeat of a ravenous beast. I've slain at least six dozen of these before, but I exercise care, my sword blacked with oil, my footsteps quieter than any assassin's stride.

I stopped before the door to this two-room abode. I closed my eyes, concentrating, extending my gloved hand upon the door, but not daring to touch it. The taint of evil is real and can penetrate velvet as a sword can punch through paper. The last thing I need is to become corrupted like these monsters.

Satisfied I felt no imminent danger, I chanted the hex, gesturing to the door, and it opened in utter silence. Darkness greeted me though I heard the sounds of soft snoring within, the inhabitants unaware of the horrible danger they were in. Or were they a part of the plot? I often granted the benefit of a doubt unless evidence presents itself otherwise.

I entered and found the room where my prey slept. With another wave of my hand, the door opened, the grip on my sword tight. I dashed, not daring it any chance to awake.

In a fluid motion, I brought my blade down in one fierce thrust! I ended the threat, blood staining the sheets. I uttered a sigh as I completed my task, and the good people of the Black Lands shall rest easier this night knowing saints like me keep them safe! Praise my beloved Empress, the Obsidian Goddess! I know she blesses me.

Light flooded into the nursery. A scream pierced the silence. "My child! My child! Gods above, no! He was only an infant, you vile monster!"

Another sword thrust and the mother who birthed this abomination fell to the floor, clutching her mortal wound before she breathed no more.

Evil manifests itself in many ways. It is a festering cancer, growing to a bloody bulbous proportion. I must be vigilant. I must be the Hand of Justice, for I am the *Crea'dynl*, the sanctified Inquisitor, ordained by the Empress, the Obsidian Goddess, herself!

Prophecy

Vijayaraj Mahendraraj

"Are you certain?"

"Yes, visions never lie. Young prince, you are the prophesied. Have faith and deliver us from this tyranny," replied the blind prophet.

Thus, the prince and his army of rebels, outnumbered and ill-trained, stormed the capital with the will of the gods. Not one of them reached the gates, for the trap was sprung and the bodies were innumerable.

"Your money and a safe bit of land, as promised. You did well," declared the emissary.

As the prophet passed the rebel prince, choking on blood, he remarked, "Visions never lie, but their vessels do what they must."

THE HIBAGON

Jasiah Witkofsky

Kiyoi was a lovely girl, yet the corpse on the bark-laden ground was anything but beautiful. Her dead eyes bulged far beyond the coverings of her veined lids and her forearm was rent, completely removed from the elbow joint. The bruise upon her neck was so large it crawled up her lower jaw and swelled at the delicate pit formed between her collarbones. Katai could not determine the exact cause of death; strangulation, the gory delimbing, or sheer terror starkly etched upon her bloated pupils.

The blue-robed samurai rose from his investigations, motioning his retainers to attend the body. His men worked in silence, knowing well not to question the master when his brow furrowed in contemplation. With arms hidden inside voluminous sleeves, he led the sombre procession back to the village.

* * *

Kiyoi was the fourth victim to succumb from such bestial attacks since the monsoon season ended. A decree had been called: no one was to leave the outer gates without accompaniment. The cold had come early this cycle, and the dawns brought a faint dusting of snow that vanished upon the hour of the horse. When the Sun Goddess, Amaterasu, made her appearance, she could not warm the hearts of her underlings upon the terrestrial plane.

Masanori Katai, freshly purified from a scalding bath, entered the austere Mitaki temple to find the clarity of Amida Buddha. A bald monk bowed and accepted the noble warrior into the wooden hall. Sitting upon his heels, Katai relinquished his *daisho* to the floor; the dual swords constant to his attire since manhood. The monk lit incense, but the samurai's posture never slouched. The only movement came from deep, rhythmic breaths, and thoughts that traversed possibilities of the future. No-mind could not be attained, but it made no matter, for his decision had been made. Affixing his blades to his sash, Katai departed the dim chamber, passing the old monk raking autumn leaves from the twisted gravel path.

The swordsman trekked his way to the seaside, skirting the net and pole fishermen who dotted the coastline. Brisk steps brought him to the ferryman, who he paid to take him to the nearest island. The gentle lap of the plum-hued sea cradling the silhouettes of merchant ships brought a vision of serene tranquillity that could not disrupt the discipline of a man on a mission. Upon landing, Katai ordered the seafarer to await his return and carefully paced the slick stones of the jagged beach to the rugged interior.

Rustic huts became visible through wind-scarred trunks and the island folk bowed, almost fearfully, as the mainland representative made his way to the last of the ramshackle structures. The sojourner was about to knock upon the entrance when he spotted the familiar old woman watering rocks around the corner of the building. Frowning, he turned to face the huddled elder. "Still feeding your pets, Mother?"

Turning a seamed face to her son, she beamed a wide smile. "How do you think they stay so healthy…like you, my boy? It is always most pleasant to see you well, Katai."

"As it is to see you, *Okaasan*." The look on his face told a different tale. He turned to the stunted yew tree at his side as if appreciating its chaotic form.

"What brings you here, son? Have you given your Anzen another child?"

He popped a stiff needle off the tiny tree. "No, *Okaasan*, not yet…"

The matron was too wise to miss the disappointment in his monotone. "So what truly brings you to me? I see purpose in your posture."

He faced the weathered visage of the woman who bore him. "Have you heard of what happened back home?"

"How could I not? My ears are younger than my years. And the fisher folk do not have much else to gossip of."

She rose from her stone-tending to fully engage her progeny. "Come to your point, my boy. When you are not straight, you are either angry or scared. I know your evasions, Katai."

Annoyed, he flicked at a miniscule leaf at his feet. "I am responsible for the domain, *Okaasan*. And I know not what kills our people. There are no bears in the area for a thousand years, yet no human can cause the savagery I have seen. I must stop whatever is committing these unholy atrocities."

"Oh Katai. You never could accept a mystery. Never sleeping until you solved a dilemma. It's what makes you such a worthy bladesman. Like the katana, you cut through to completion."

"*Okaasan!* Your poetry does not help the situation." Frustrated, he broke his poise to grip her shoulders.

"Let the *hatamoto* handle this." She responded.

"Our Lord is old. I am the strongest in the village. This is my sworn duty." He released her and smoothed her sleeves gently. "Mother, come back with me. I cannot protect you if you are not near."

"No son. With the passing of your father, I have decided to return here to my birthplace. There are good reasons for this. You live under the shadow of Mount Hiba, which will always be a land of sorrow and tragedy. Since the beginning of time when Great Goddess Izanami died giving birth to Fire and was buried beneath the mountain. Now there are monsters. In time, Sunfire will rain down from the sky to land on Hiroshima, bringing countless deaths and untold suffering. You live on cursed land, brave Katai, and it would be favourable if you brought your family here to escape this madness."

"You know I cannot do that, *Okaasan*." He turned from his mother, brooding, "Your superstitious Shinto pales beneath the light of rational Buddha. I know of the steps I must take."

"So much like your sire. So stubborn and outward seeing." She placed a reassuring palm up the small of his back. "If only I could have shared more of my insight. If only you saw my stories as more than mere fables for children." A single thin river ran the creases of her time-ravaged cheek.

Over his shoulder, Katai gave his mother one last glance. "*Okaasan*...I implore you. Reclaim your room at our estate. All lands face trouble, but at home I can ease those burdens. Please...come."

"I am of more service here than assuming the role of a frail invalid to be preened over." She withdrew her hand from her son's immovable spine.

He turned back to the path. "When I return, I shall bear better news...and hopefully a son." The samurai began retracing his steps. "Farewell, *Okaasan*."

The return journey neared closure when Masanori Katai's nostrils were assailed by the reek of stale and rotting death. Around a wooded bend, the *bushi* found his way obstructed by the carcass of a mutilated ox. One side of the bovine's torso was gnawed away by a maw larger than any carnivore found upon the isles of the Rising Sun.

Despite the fading light and forest shadows, Katai's keen eyes discerned a single track imprinted upon the gore-soaked mud. He placed his foot into the indentation—twice the length and thrice the girth of his sandal. With twilight upon the horizon, the inquisitive wanderer quickened his pace homeward, his peripheral awareness activated, with one hand upon the hilt of his long sword.

The training session bore an intensity uncommon to the practice field. The *clack-clack-clacking* of the hardwood *bokken* used in place of sharpened steel could be heard echoing against stone and bamboo walls. The mock duels were abruptly interrupted by the hurried approach of an *ashigaru* guard.

"There's been another attack. You all must come, quickly!"

The cadre of warriors rushed out of the interior gates with oaken weapons in hand. Villagers crowded around two woodsmen supporting an old man with dark blood matted to the side of his scalp. Katai pushed his way into the throng of peasants to face the shaky form of Gimu, the herb gatherer. The indentation that generated the crimson smear on his thin white hair erased any optimism for the elder's continued longevity.

Lifting the jaw of the semi-conscious man, Katai forced eye contact with his dying gaze. "Gimu…stay with me. You must tell me what happened."

One of the men carrying the wounded senior chimed

in, "Forgive me, Master. We went out this morning to gather firewood and Gimu separated to gather moss. When we heard his screams, we found him like this."

Katai neared, nose to nose with the fading soul he cradled. "What happened? Who did this to you?"

Gimu inhaled a rattling breath to gasp out his final words. "Monster…the Hibagon!"

* * *

Katai arose before the sun to mate with his wife. The passion of his grip and movements was atypical of such a restrained man. Upon completion, he sat at the edge of the bedding, unfolding his thickest kimono from a nearby cubby.

His spouse rolled towards him to lay a serene hand on the tense muscles of his back, gently caressing the overcorrect posture.

"So…today is the day that you must leave."

"Yes." He rose to cinch on the broadcloth attire of his station. "The moon is full, and I must scale Mount Hiba before the snows come in full. It is the only logical hideout for the killer. No more need die, Anzen, my treasure. You must understand the necessity of this."

She lay back and pulled the coverings to shield herself from the brisk air. "You were strong with me in our joining. It is also my time of fertility. I think you planted a son inside me."

A slight smile broke through his stoic features. "That would be most fortuitous, a blessing from Amida."

Anzen shivered beneath the sheets. “In order for a sword to forge true, a master smith must be there to shape the metal…same with a father and son.”

“So now you are an expert on metal making? Do not succumb to the fear of the peasants—it is unbecoming of you. Besides, I do not make this trek alone.” He finished tying the topknot at the crown of his skull and grabbed the swords from the lacquered stand that elegantly displayed the tools of the trade. Katai rose from the bed and kneaded her calves through the downy blankets. “Find more sleep, my treasure. I shall return home with the head of a murderer and there will be no need for any more worry.”

As the sky began to blue, Katai crossed to the nearest room and carefully opened the sliding door. His vision adjusted to the dim light, revealing the outline of his sleeping daughter. Seven summers of age and as beautiful as her mother. He brushed a night-black lock from her round face. The skin was warm with life in the chill morning, and the most vivid memories of her flooded his being. Her first birth cry entering the world, the squeal she gave running her thumb along the razor edge of his blade, the raucous laughter she generated from the spectators when a toad she caught leapt from her hands to land full on his face.

The reason for his entire way of being. He grew ever harder, firm like a rock to protect the softness of others. This was not done out of pity or derision, for the best things he knew were gentle, fragile, delicate. His mother, wife, daughter, the meek folk of his humble village…all depended on him to stay solid, sharp, true. A philosophy that squared perfectly with his inheritance as samurai; a noble warrior to serve his lord and those beneath him. Why he drove those who shared his rank so diligently, to force the impurities out so only virtuous essence remained.

Duty brought him back to the present moment, and with a final graze across his cub's cheek, he turned and left.

* * *

The party of four reached the base of the mountains as the sun peaked full. The pathway split east and west, wrapping around both sides of the gigantic earthen protrusion…the fabled mountain named Hiba. Katai sent Tetsu and Kuma along the left-hand trail while he and Usagi took the opposite route.

As the way escalated, the evergreens and beech trees began to thin, giving way for the chaparral and dried grass that covered the smooth face of the mountainside. Katai let Usagi take the lead, for no one knew the mountain better than his wiry companion. The sun began to near the horizon when the two samurai reached a point where the land's features became craggier and more fissured. The duo halted for a repast of water and rice balls.

"Usagi, I would like you to stay here and start a fire." Katai said, splashing some liquid on his hands to scrub off the sticky paste from his fingers. "I will explore further."

Usagi stared at his taller comrade, wide-eyed. "We should not separate. That is the rule!"

"The rule is for farmers and wash women. We are

armed men." Katai tightened his sash. "It should not take me long, and I need you here to prepare a camp."

"This is foolish! Too much is unknown, and caution is wise in these dangerous times. You must listen to me, you stubborn goat!" Usagi implored his friend.

Katai checked the positioning of his blades and turned towards his destination. "If I do not come back by moonrise, I need you to return home to amass a larger contingency. This threat must be vanquished."

"The people all speak of a monster. What else could kill so savagely?"

"The fear of the superstitious has entered your heart, Usagi. There are no monsters…and if so, they are still flesh enough to die by steel." With that, Katai strode off towards the mountain top.

* * *

Measured steps advanced through a ravine carved into the terrain by eons of rainfall. If this was a typical military campaign, Katai would have ordered Usagi to scout the enemy's position. Since the circumstances were anything but typical, Katai chose to proceed on his own, for he was never one to sacrifice another on his own account. Buddha taught the interdependence of all beings, and Katai saw that truth from the highest lord to the lowliest filth cleaner.

Masanori Katai spread his visual acuity to the peripheries, the situational awareness of the hunter fully activated, ready to absorb any sight or sound out of the ordinary. Despite this state of heightened focus, the swordsman barely managed to avoid the debris which exploded forth from a hurled boulder.

Looking to the source of the violent disturbance, Katai beheld the silhouette of a broad, man-shaped figure huffing hoarsely above. With a tremendous lunge, the aggressor landed hulkingly on the path behind the samurai. Nearly doubling the height of a fully grown man, the creature's entire body was covered with dark, thick bristles, stiff and spiny like the mane of a boar. All four limbs ended with immense hands that could easily clutch a person by the chest. The nails protruding from each digit were hardened and sharp as claws, like the talons on a falcon. Yet the most frightful trait rested above the apelike maw…the dark eyes of a cognisant human radiating pure animosity.

With a smooth, swift flick of the arm, Katai released the katana from its enamelled sheath and took a wide stance, facing the beast. The monstrosity took no notice of the weapon as it tore a small stump from the side of the ravine. Katai stepped in at this moment and allowed his left shoulder to take the grazing blow of the thrown log as he slashed into the massive torso. The monster stumbled back, clutching its stomach as Katai tried to ignore the throbbing in his arm. He took reassurance from the crimson droplets shed from his blade…the giant was mortal.

Taking advantage of his opponent's pain, Katai unleashed a sweeping overhead slash. Unnatural reflexes halted the katana's momentum, as the beast rapidly clutched the sword hand of its prey. The enormous, muscle-strewn arm hoisted the significantly smaller captive off his feet, and as the grip tightened, Katai could hear the bones of his hand shatter above his moans of pain.

In desperation, Katai drew the shorter *wakizashi* from its scabbard and plunged the tip below the collarbone of his captor. The savage humanoid revealed its fanged incisors as it produced a strange sucking gasp and tossed the samurai into the dirt like a child throws a doll. Katai watched the large entity whimper off through the dust before shock and wind loss faded consciousness into darkness.

Katai awoke on the rocks, spitting grime and gravel from his parched mouth. Groaning, he forced himself to his knees. He looked down at the mangled shape of his hand, clutching the sword hilt in a death grip that would not open. Awkwardly tearing strips from the sleeve of his kimono, Katai almost blacked out once again whilst cinching the straps around the ruined fingers, solidifying the hold on his weapon. Struggling to his feet, Katai could make out the gore droplets of his bestial foe in the fading light. Shuffling forth in gritted determination, the lone warrior proceeded onward with single-minded purpose.

It did not take long for the weary fighter to find the object of his pursuit. The beast frantically tore at the short sword protruding from its heaving breast outside the crevice from which Katai emerged. A series of snorts from the upturned snout brought the monster's attention to the bedraggled figure approaching. Ignoring the invasive steel, it rose to square off with the advancing intruder.

The samurai drew upon the last vestiges of his energy for one final gamble. His pace quickened gradually into a full sprint, straight at his target. The beast held its arms akimbo, breathing hard and staring forward as if in a ritualistic trance. Before Katai could get within arm's length of the beast's massive reach, he lunged, bringing the moon-gleaming blade down in a two-handed arc, exhaling the warrior's shout to shatter his enemy's resolve.

Usagi rose upon hearing the battle cry off in the distance, followed by a tremendous growl unlike any sound to have ever reached his sharp ears.

An internal debate ensued within the frantic mind of the solitary watchman. Travel farther up the Hiba to assist Katai or heed the man's words to inform the village. A crisis of loyalty, help his sworn companion or deliver his dire message and abandon his overconfident superior to the night. The latter option felt like cowardice, as did the indecision which rooted him in place, stuck like a prisoner in limbo. And there was no way to find Tetsu and Kuma at this stage in the hunt.

The reverie was broken when a single extended cry erupted through the stillness of the moment. Another animalistic bellow joined the first, and then there were many forming a chorus, as wolves do when they open their jaws to the moon. The eerie, atonal song was fierce, angry, and carried a hint of sadness, which drove terror into Usagi's paralysed heart.

Instinct overcame valorous discipline as Usagi cut a mad dash down the slope by illumination of the lunar orb. At full speed, he ran to warn the villagers, but there was no need. Like the roar of the lion, the frightful cacophony could be heard down the mountain and over the sea.

5-4-3-2-1

D.L. Shirey

What did the shrink say? That trick when I feel overwhelmed. 5-4-3-2-1. Focus on senses, turn off my brain and stop obsessing. Just stop.

5-4-3-2-1.

Okay, take a breath; concentrate on where I am right now. Five things I see: wet pavement, trash, syringes, a dumpster, #6 spray-painted on the wall.

Touch four things—why are my hands sticky? Stop. Four things: extension cord, my inhaler, soiled bedsheets, a high heel. No shoe, just the heel.

Three things I hear: sirens, dog barking, the whispers.

Two things I smell: piss, cheap perfume.

One taste: that perfume.

I'm feeling better already.

RED SKY'S MORNING

Daniel R. Robichaud

"When these pirates board," Captain Karin said as the enemy airship's grapnel lines caught hold, "you slash, you kick, you do whatever needs doing to dump the *Caucus*'s scum over the side. Let them contemplate their errs while plummeting into the Deathly Valley. Let their smashed bones tell cautionary tales: no corsairs will ever take the *Anastasia*. Her cargo is safe, her crew is the finest, and her skyways mastery is undisputed."

Swords and fists pumped the air, accompanied by zealous cheers.

Karin made the first killing cut herself. Her blade opened a *Caucus* man before his soles touched the *Anastasia*'s deck. His dying agonies invigorated Karin's crew.

Clashing swords threw sparks. Flintlock censers spat gunpowder incense and valedictions. Howls sounded across the deck, voicing rage, battle lust, blood frenzy, dying agonies, and the *Anastasia*'s ultimate victory.

The *Caucus* fled until the *Anastasia*'s cannons boomed. A well-placed ball ruptured the enemy vessel's steam engines. Explosions ripped the galleon to pieces.

"Cap'n?" First Mate Bordeaux said. "These men beg mercy and offer to serve."

Seven pirates knelt, hands atop their crowns.

She gestured to the strongest lout. "What's your name?"

"David." His face was a gargantuan infant's—pouting lips and wide eyes, and not a hint of guile. "Some call me Dumb."

"Have Dumb David here tie knots to prove his value," she said. "The rest?" A smile cracked her scarred face. "Because of Philomela's virtue, the gods transformed her into a bird so she might be spared destruction. Let these men trust their virtue to grow them wings."

"You harpy," a rat faced man said. "May the Death Frigate find you, and—"

"You should pray to saviours, not fables." Karin waved a dismissing hand. Her airmen's boots launched the pirates shrieking overboard.

Afterward, Bordeaux reported, "Not one virtuous man among them."

* * *

Before week's end, Bordeaux said, "Dumb David is a fine catch. He's born to this work. His affinity with knots is damned near supernatural. Despite his bulk, he scales rigging faster than anyone else."

"And his cunning?" she asked.

"He's been noggin struck once too often," Bordeaux said. "He possesses little sense. Take this conversation:

"Knowing your preference, I asked him about tattoos. He said he had one. 'Uh-oh,' I said, 'Show us.' He pulled open his shirt, baring his breast. Not a tattoo, it was a birthmark!" Bordeaux laughed, then grew thoughtful. "It was queer, though."

"Explain."

"Its shape..." Bordeaux splayed fingers on his left hand. "Like a bloody handprint. Like he bargained with something horrible. Or whatever land bound wretches sired him did. Have you heard the stories of the damned born...?"

"Keep alert for trouble."

Bordeaux scratched the brow above his eye patch. "Of course, Cap'n."

* * *

Nine days after their victory over the *Caucus*, as morning haemorrhaged across the heavens, the *Anastasia* found herself pursued.

Karin's telescope revealed the ship was an unserviceable ruin, belching as much smoke as steam. The gas bag showed a dozen poor patch efforts. Her skeleton crew worked with manic intensity. Burns and gouges obliterated the galleon's name, leaving *Lethe*.

"What rusted hulk is this?" Bordeaux asked. "Think she survived pirates?"

"She needs aid," Karin said. "Slow engines, and—"

"*We can't*," a third man said.

"I don't recall asking your opinion, Dumb David."

"I'm terribly sorry, Captain, but that ship—she's not looking for help."

"A wounded bird," Bordeaux said, "inviting prey?"

Karin said, "We'll not lose our cargo—"

"They don't want cargo," Dumb David said. His birthmark must have itched furiously, from the way he scratched his shirt.

"Come on you lummox—"

Dumb David yanked his arm free from Bordeaux's grip. "Captain. They will reach us."

"Are you smoke crazed?" Bordeaux asked. "That thing's not flying. It's crashing at two knots."

Karin discovered something new in Dumb David's eyes. Understanding. Knowledge. Whatever idiocy had earned his nickname had passed, revealing a heretofore hidden sage.

"Speak your mind," Karin said.

"The Death Frigate—"

"Is a fable, Mr David."

"Her crew," Dumb David said, indicating the *Lethe* with a nod, "is blood crazed. Once they've scented prey, no power on earth will dissuade them."

"We are heavens bound," she observed. "Perhaps our dissuasions are more convincing?" Dumb David's response was a grim frown.

"Shall I call for slow engines, Cap'n?"

"Full steam, instead. Also, please restore Mr David here to whatever task he's abandoned for our 'enlightenment'. And Mr Bordeaux?"

"Yes?"

"Have the men prepare for boarders though such preparations might well be useless..."

"Affirmative, Cap'n."

* * *

The *Lethe* had more to her than expected. In under an hour, she overcame the *Anastasia*. Snarling, drooling, raving men wearing dried blood war paint peopled her crew. To look upon them was to see raw ferocity, to gaze into madness incarnate.

Karin's sabre indicated the ship when she addressed her crew. "We've met scum before. That is all we face now. Their dress is fearsome, but they are men.

"The *Anastasia*'s skyways mastery is indisputable. We will not be turned aside by this wretched dozen."

The *Lethe*'s grapnels arrived, and her crew swung over. Karin struck first, slashing an opponent's belly without reward. The *Lethe*'s men's skin was iron hard. With a snarl, the grizzled boarder swung his gaff like a quarterstaff. She parried and stabbed his heart, but the man ignored this blow.

The *Anastasia*'s men panicked—this enemy was invulnerable and deadly fighters.

"The eyes," Dumb David called. "*Aim for their eyes*."

Karin's flintlock came to hand, and she fired into her opponent's face, closing his eye with a bullet. The boarder collapsed.

"The devils' eyes are their weakness!" With Dumb David's direction, the *Anastasia*'s crew repelled the supernatural invaders. Victory came costly, though. Twelve boarders had killed almost twenty men.

"You're a fine catch, Mr David," Karin said. "How are you so familiar with devils?" However, as the *Lethe* dwindled in their view, Dumb David's eyes clouded once more. His preternatural knowledge passed, and the imbecile remained. "What a mystery you are, Mr David."

LAST WORDS FOR THE DRAGONSLAYER

Nathan Slemp

So, you've killed me, 'hero.' Congratulations. What now for my eggs?

Will you abandon them? Ah, but dragonets are vengeful, and mine know your scent. You would not escape them. Smashing their eggs won't spare you, either. Their souls are vengeful too.

Or will you save yourself by adopting them? Ah, but raising dragons… it changes you, as you change them. You would lose something of yourself, gain something of dragonhood instead. An exchange of natures. An evolution.

Either way, your life as you know it ended when your blade pierced my chest. So which end will you choose, "hero?"

THE SORCERER'S SKY

Sheldon Woodbury

The pounding hooves on the forest floor thudded gloomily in the foggy night air. The distant sound was coming from three different directions, one from the towering mountains in the north, the other from the swampy lowlands in the south, and the last from a more secret location somewhere between the other two.

The night sky was the same as always, splattered with stars that looked as if they'd been thrown into the heavens by an angry god. In the sprawling woods below, the fog was the way it always was, too—a thick black mist slithering through the colossal trees and covering the barren ground like a ghostly shroud.

Ever since the Great War, the massive forest had been shunned and avoided whenever possible. There were whispered rumours that the ground below was not just layers of earth and rock, but a hidden region of unknown horrors. There were other rumours too, all of them whispered in the same hushed tone.

But on this night, important business needed to be attended to, and the gathering participants were not the fearful sort. They'd chosen secrecy and privacy over rumoured terrors.

The pounding hooves grew closer, and now there was a clear distinction between them. From the blustery north it was a single galloping that was steady and fierce, from the warmer south a much greater flurry of charging sounds, while the last was another solitary mount clopping along at a much slower gait.

A giant beast like horse was the first to appear, bursting in between two twisted trees, its flaring nostrils snorting in the foggy night air. It was carrying an equally mammoth rider encased in bulky armour of forged steel that made him seem like a metal god. Deadly weapons cut from the same steel clattered and clacked on both sides of the panting beast.

A harnessed team galloped in next, pulling a carriage that glittered like a crimson jewel in the misty fog. It had soaring spires of polished gold on each corner of its bevelled roof, and silver crusted wheels that flashed out lightning-like sparks.

They waited in silence until the last footfalls finally clopped in, but the animal that appeared was more like a scrawny mule, so exhausted at the end of the journey it wouldn't be able to make the trip back home.

Perched on its back was a shadowy figure hunched over with the accumulated miseries of old age. He was draped in a simple black cloak that was unadorned, his long, tangled hair the colour of the palest full moon. The old man climbed off his ride with halting efforts, trembling with weakness, until he was finally standing unsteadily on the ground.

The rider bounded off his massive beast with ease and tugged off his helmet with the same easy swiftness. A mane of black hair tumbled out, falling around his brutishly handsome face and arrogant eyes. He wasn't a god, but he had the haughty sneer of someone who'd accept the role if given.

The door to the ornate red carriage creaked open next, revealing the final attendant for this midnight meeting. A woman of startling beauty appeared, stepping slowly down to the dark forest ground. Her attire was the exact opposite of the other two, nothing but sheer red silk caressing her body like shimmering skin. Her hair was the colour of fire, her eyes like the first shadow of night.

"Let's get right to business," the man snapped.

"I agree," the woman purred.

"As you wish," the old man wheezed, pulling his black cloak tighter around him. In the darkness of night and the strangling fog, he seemed to be barely there.

The armoured man lowered his voice, but it retained its steely sharpness. "As the newly appointed leader of the Mendalok Kingdom, I assure you I come with the total allegiance of my people."

The old man gazed back with a look of frail curiosity. "What's your name, young man?" he wheezed, pulling off the hood of his draping black cloak. "My apologies if we've already met. The years are starting to steal away some of my precious faculties, and I need to make sure I know what I need to do."

The man chuckled, but it was more like a dismissive taunt. "But aren't you the great and glorious wizard that the legends all prattle on about? Can't you just mumble a few silly magical words and pluck my name out of thin air?"

The old wizard shrugged, and even this seemed to take more physical effort than it should. He was shivering, his thin cloak fluttering around him.

"Let's get on with it," the woman purred, brushing away a fallen lock of her fiery hair.

Even in the night darkness and the thick black mist, it was easy to see her shimmery allure was not lost on the man, nor his brawny presence on her.

"You, I remember," the wizard mumbled, gazing at the woman with his milky-white eyes. "Mistress Kantrell, the eternally beautiful Queen of the Ryling Kingdom."

The stars in the night sky seemed to flicker for an instant, their brightness weakening for a moment, but the eyes below were unaware.

The armoured man marched closer to the wobbly old wizard.

"We asked for this meeting because it's time for a change. After the Great War, your kingdom of sorcerers was granted supremacy over ours. We've acceded to your rule without rancour or resistance, but the time has come to take measure of what we've gotten in return."

The wizard gazed back with a stronger effort to concentrate. He clutched his old hands in front of him, his milky eyes a shade whiter than his tangled long hair.

"We have given you the benefit of our magic," he murmured softly.

The man took another stride closer. "What magic is that? We have toiled our own fields and rebuilt our own dwellings, all without your help. The Great War was a long time ago, and we can't keep living in the past. It's time for a change. It's time for new blood."

"What do you remember of the Great War?" the wizard wheezed, clenching his tattered black robe around his frail body. He held his ground, not showing the slightest hint of fear to the much bulkier figure now looming in front of him.

The man hesitated. "I was young at the time, so just what I've heard. My mother told me the stories. Many were killed, much was destroyed."

"And you?" the wizard asked, turning his weary gaze to the beautiful queen.

"The same," she replied. "Just what I've heard from the legends in the palace when I was a child. It was a time of great bloodshed and death."

"Yes," the wizard murmured, gazing down at the dark forest floor. "There has been no war like it since the earliest of times. But the death and destruction were far beyond what even the legends proclaim. Our rule is because of that war. Our magic is needed for the times we live in..."

The giant night sky flickered with the same quick flash of dimness, but again, it was not seen by the eyes below.

The beautiful queen stepped closer too. "My kingdom agrees it's time for a change. We believe in pursuing all the pleasures of life. Under our rule, we'll usher in a glorious new age."

A look of anger came to the man's brutish face. "I disagree. My people are clearly more suited to rule. We believe in the rewards of hard work and discipline, a purity of body and spirit."

The old wizard gazed back with growing impatience. He looked like he was about to doze off, still standing hunched on his feet. "So, you have no need of my magic anymore?"

The man snorted with barely concealed contempt. "Let's be honest, old man, your silly little tricks are best suited for the amusement of children and scared old hags who need something to believe in. As you can see, we are neither."

One of the giant horses brayed and stomped its great hooves on the ground. It was now the other side of midnight, and the slithering mist seemed to gather around them in a tighter swirl.

"I have heard your wishes, but my answer is no," the wizard muttered with the same weary voice. He nodded a droopy goodbye and turned his sagging body to go.

"Hold your ground, old man!" the armoured man

bellowed in a voice that sounded like a braying beast. He thrust his hand out and grabbed the wizard's sagging shoulder, spinning him back around. "I see that I have to be more direct." They were face-to-face again, but the frail wizard still showed no signs of fear. The look in his milky old eyes betrayed nothing but the tiniest hint of mystery.

The brutish man yanked his sword from the leather sheath at his side, the long blade glinting in the darkness. The sweeping night sky flickered again, but still they didn't see it.

Then, a quick moment later, they did see this—

Suddenly, in the swirling fog around them, fearsome creatures began to appear, seeming to take monstrous form out of the night mist itself. There were towering ogres as tall as the trees, and giant worm-like creatures oozing through the fog. The ogres howled like banshees, and the giant worm-like creatures spewed out billowing gusts of flapping bats.

The beautiful queen stumbled back, her face turning to a shade very close to the wizard's milky-white gaze. But now it was the man who showed no hint of fear, or trembling sign of intimidation. He stood in front of the howling terror coming at them and shoved his sword back in its sheath.

"Well done, old man," he chuckled. "So, the legends are true. Your sorcery is great indeed. But it's still a trick, an imaginary concoction that isn't there."

The cutting words seemed to hit the old wizard with an invisible force. He let out a moan, as if a part of what was keeping him alive seeped out too.

The fearsome creatures slowly turned back into foggy mist, then swirled away into nothingness.

And now the man glared back with even more brutish anger. “You continue to treat me with no respect. I told you it’s time for new blood, but first we need to get rid of the blood that’s old...”

The man rammed his sword into the wizard’s chest, twisted it savagely, then shoved his old body backwards to the ground. The wizard lay in a trembling heap, gazing up at his killer with dying white eyes.

“So be it,” he muttered. “But also know this. When I die, my magic dies too...”

The beautiful queen stared down at the fallen body in shocked surprise, but only for a moment.

“So be it, indeed,” she purred, strolling to the man still holding the blood-soaked sword. She reached out and took his other hand with a soft caress. “There’s still the matter of who’s going to rule. Let’s go back to my palace and discuss it in more pleasurable surroundings.”

The man smiled, nodding his assent.

They were clopping away inside the glittering carriage when the old wizard wheezed out his final breath, and this is when the illusion it had taken all his skill and strength to conjure began to crumble away too. It was like the thick mist was suddenly parting, revealing what had really been there all along. They heard crunching and snapping beneath the carriage’s silver crusted wheels. They both turned to the window and instantly saw a startling sight.

Outside was now a different world.

The foggy forest was gone.

Now they were in an endless field completely covered with crumbled white skeletons, a gruesome necropolis left over from the Great War. The star-splattered heavens disappeared too, becoming a black sky, churning with the ashes of death. The old wizard was telling the truth. The Great War was even worse than the legends had said, because this is what had really been left behind.

Then the beautiful queen and the brutish warrior discovered even they weren't completely real. The queen's beautiful face and figure crumbled away too, along with the man's bulk and brawn. The brutal truth was they were both malnourished, feeble shadows of what they'd looked like before. Because this had been part of the wizard's spell too, to hide the physical ravages of those who'd managed to survive and live in a world they believed was real.

As the carriage crunched over the sea of bones, they now saw their world the way it really was—a devastated wasteland haunted by the past. It was more a home for the dead than a home for the living, and it would always be that way. That's why the kingdom of sorcerers had been put in charge, because sometimes the magical is better than what's real.

An Unexpected Guest

Toko Hata

The snow had kept falling for weeks. With most of the corpses hidden in a silver veil, the world appeared heartbreakingly beautiful; it almost flaunted a hallucination of the better days.

Today, an unknown girl arrived in front of the tribe. Though her features were barely visible because of her thick scarf, the pattern on her wrist signified noble origin.

"I have brought back your kin," she stated.

With those words, they noticed the dampness of her bag, the unnatural shape crammed into it. Behind her was a bloody trail—engraved onto the blank snow, the scarlet colour still fresh.

THE WEIGHT OF ONE

R. Wayne Gray

The night felt no fear in their presence as they huddled in the slight grove of maple trees. Crickets kept up a steady chorus around them as bats swooped overhead, their foraging only apparent when they passed in front of the oversized full moon.

Ptei fought memories, tried to keep his focus on the old farmhouse that sat down the road in shade. Hadn't he sat like this as a child; under the stars, his sense of self absorbed by its massive presence? It seemed very familiar, and Ptei had actually grown up but one state away, so everything from the scent of flowers to the buzz of specific insects only fed the old scenes playing in his head.

And he was doing it again. Ptei shook his head and brought the binoculars up to his eyes. The farmhouse leapt at him, moonlit surfaces fading to shadows and blackness. He tapped a button atop the binoculars and night vision bathed the farmhouse in a false light, highlighting missing boards, crumbling walls, and the partially collapsed roof of a barn.

It also showed a thin grey line drifting out of the chimney, but he already knew that. He breathed in, a hint of smoke on the cool country air.

Saba put a hand on his shoulder, and he placed one finger atop the back of it.

Just a minute.

He pushed the button one more time, and several bright bursts of yellow suddenly appeared amid the darkness of the farmhouse. One danced lively near the outer wall, a small fire set in a hearth, the chimney above it glowing a dull yellow.

The other two yellow areas appeared to be seated at a kitchen table. They were human shaped.

Ptei watched for several more seconds and then turned back to her. Returning the binoculars to a pocket in his coat, he grasped Saba's hands and started silently signing.

Two in all. Eating in the kitchen.

No dogs?

Just the two. Front or back?

Back. Remember: it's her we want.

Not my first rodeo. Be careful.

Saba squeezed his hands, and then lightly touched his cheek. In her other hand, she made a fist and extended it three times.

Fifteen.

She touched her wrist, the red glow from a watch

briefly giving definition to the trees around them. Patting him on the shoulder, she silently slipped out of the tree grove.

Fifteen minutes later, Ptei came in hard through the front while Saba crept in through the back. The front door slammed against the wall, startling the couple who sat in a candlelit pool of light at the table. They were young, barely out of their teens. The girl screamed and raised her hands, while the boy toppled over backwards in his chair, rolling towards the mattress laid out on the kitchen floor.

He never made it. Saba moved quickly from the rear porch, intercepting him as he reached for the shotgun leaning against the wall near the mattress. The boy's fingers stretched and froze six inches from the gun as Saba's knife entered his throat. He dropped, fifteen seconds of wet, whooshing gasps his last sounds before he settled onto the floor with a sigh.

The girl froze when the knife entered the boy's throat but, as he exhaled his last, the shock broke and she screamed. She leaped to her feet and started across the kitchen, making it but a few steps before Ptei clubbed her with the butt of his handgun. She dropped to the floor, her arm coming to rest across the body of the boy.

* * *

When the girl came to, two monsters were standing over her. She gasped, an intake of air that ended as a low moan as she remembered the dead boy. She couldn't see him from this angle, tied as she was to the kitchen table.

The larger monster leaned in close, and she felt a needle enter her arm. He was human, but his face was swollen, his skin red and covered in rotting patches that oozed a black liquid.

"You have Findlay Syndrome," the girl said. He leaned forward and back, which she took to be a nod. He didn't really need to confirm it; the look of the both of them, the smell, the fact that they didn't talk. Findlay Syndrome.

"You didn't have to kill him. He was normal," she said, her voice breaking. The larger monster held up the device that he had stabbed her with. Its lights and numbers were meaningless to her, but she knew what it meant: immune.

She started to protest, but the smaller monster was already stabbing her with a much larger needle.

And then pain, and then blackness.

* * *

Ptei rinsed black residue from the two collapsible cups and stored them away in the duffel bag. Saba was across the kitchen, staring into a small mirror over the sink and playing with her hair, stroking her smooth cheek. He walked over and rested his hands on her shoulders.

"You look better," Ptei said.

Saba smiled. "Yeah, for a few weeks, anyways." She tapped at the watch on her wrist, which cast a green glow into the kitchen. They both turned to the kitchen table where the desiccated remains of the girl—minus two fingers—lay. "Just a girl."

"No different from any of the others. Taste-wise, anyways," Ptei said. Saba glared at him, and he held up his hands in surrender.

"Too soon, I know. I hate it too. But her sacrifice will keep 1000 people back home well for another couple of months. At which time, hopefully we will have found another. Top or bottom?"

Saba grabbed the feet while Ptei strapped on the duffel and grasped the girl's shoulders. As she did every time, Saba marvelled at how light a body was after you got done removing all the water from it for transport.

Loverboy

Birgit K. Gaiser

Sprawling on the chaise longue, looking every inch the part of an artist's muse, he blinked at the queen, showing off his eyelashes.

She was feeding him grapes as if he were her superior, delighting in the roleplay. Their dalliance had gone further than intended, had become too enjoyable.

Better then, that he should stop it now. They'd had many good times, but another woman awaited him; one whose spell he could not break, not even for a queen.

He rose to stand behind her. "Greetings from your sister," he whispered through tears as his hands closed around her throat.

THE BLIND LORD AND THE HERETIC KING

Xavier Garcia

I look at him and I see all the hope of our age.

I'm not the only one who sees this, of course. It's why I was assigned to him. Why the Order sought fit to assign only the most accomplished amongst them to him.

I believe it too, obviously. That he is him, I mean. Else, I would not bend my magicks to his cause.

But even now, as I look at him, pouring himself another drink, it's obvious that I know something that neither he nor they do.

I've read the scriptures as they have. But we just don't see it the same way.

I know that the Blind Lord is coming. That belief we share in common. But that symbol, that faded vague little rune that precedes His name on the third paragraph of that rotten scroll, that ridiculous barely-there scribble on that last worn line, where they see "destroyer," I see "redeemer."

Of course, I could not tell them they were wrong, that they were interpreting the texts incorrectly. I could not admit to heresy. They wouldn't have assigned me to him if I had.

So, I sit here, in this low tavern, watching him pour himself another drink. Our future king drunk on wine, our future king with two half nude prostitutes clinging to his body and his every word.

At least he believes that they are prostitutes. It's what I led him to believe anyway. One is, sure, so at least it isn't all a lie. But the second girl, the one he's favouring, the pretty redhead who blushes when he looks at her—she's in fact, the blacksmith's wife.

I know this because I saw it happen, knew it had to happen, and so I made it so. He'll bed both girls, I know this too, and in the morning, the blacksmith and his brothers will come for him, this future king, they'll come with hammers and one may even have a sword, if I see it right, but come they will. And when they come, my future king will slay this blacksmith and his brothers, and when the woman protests and attempts to defend her newly horned husband, he'll kill her too. I know this, just as I know I'll help him bury them. Just as I know that when come his tears, I'll be there to console him, to remind him he has a larger part to play than to worry about these peasants' lives.

I need him to do these things. I need him to do much worse if he is to get to where he's going. The Blind Lord is coming. Not as destroyer but as redeemer. And when comes the Sightless God, my king will go to him, not as foe but as aid. He will take Him by the arm as one would a blind old man, and guide Him throughout His kingdom, laying waste to all corruption.

And so, I order my future king another drink.

RAIDERS

R.S. Nevil

The roar of the engines rumbled through the air.

Raiders.

The worst of the worst. The ones he tried so hard to avoid.

He had only survived this long due to his abilities. His sharpened senses the only thing keeping him alive.

Now, with the raiders bearing down on him, it seemed as though his luck had finally run out. They had found him. And they were coming for him.

There was nowhere to hide. Not as their bikes peaked over the hill, their skulled faces glaring back at him.

And he knew there would be no escape. Only pain.

THE JUNKERNAUT

William Bartlett

Morning light violated the night sky and illuminated Nyala's featureless face. The same light brightened her opponent's visage of confused horror. Nearby torchlight danced upon the creamy skin that wrapped her head's front where eyes, nose, and mouth should inhabit, but instead, only a few freckles dwelled. Blood of the sun assaulted the waking sky's serenity with a splatter, resembling Nyala's creamy knuckles as she wrapped them in burlap cloth. The night, like Nyala, foolishly resisted its daily destiny, but the light has always conquered its foes and only lets up by choice. The night never stood a chance when the sun woke, yet it fought to live just a bit longer. Nyala, unlike the night, held a hope in her favour, though it was but a sliver.

She stood ready with balled up fists, a hint of a quiver

from her face skin, and trembling legs, ready to kill a man thrice her age. Winter's first snowfall floated down from an overcast sky in friendly flakes. They disappeared on the muddy ground inside the pit. The pit was walled by crude timber logs that were sharpened at the top. Normally, the seats around the pit were filled at a challenge like this one, but not today.

"No one comes to watch your futile attempt, child," Forkav insulted through gritted teeth.

Nyala knew he was right but remained silent and ready.

"I hold forty years, girl. You hold only thirteen. You haven't even had your first blood yet. Do you..? Do you even bleed like a normal human? What manner of demon would come out of you...?" he continued through his locked jaw. "I am an Elder here! Warrior and High Warlord of this clan!"

She held her fighting stance and determined brow wrinkle firm. Forkav tossed a glance at the barbarian king, who only returned a solemn nod. Forkav shook his head in bewilderment.

"Girl…" he tried again. "I understand it is your right, and any other barbarian's right, to challenge the king for his ring, but…surely you have enough sanity left to understand your impossible chances?"

Nyala flexed without moving in response. She was tall for a thirteen-year-old girl, but nowhere near Forkav's towering seven feet. She was thin, but not without muscle. She was bald. Her skin was rich, with an eggshell hue, like a human covered in milk. Forkav's skin was darker. His hair was long and soft and bore strands of grey that crept in and out of braids. His beard was full, thick, and also braided. It was slicked with tinker grease and rolled up into a topknot in preparation for the bloodkul.

Forkav glanced at the king once again, and then at the king's right hand. They both dared not betray their stoic expressions. Forkav glared at Nyala's sponsor, a lowly mechanic.

"You old fool, what in darkness is the matter with you? How could you bring me this child? You want me to murder a girl younger than my own daughter? There is no honour in this."

"My lord," began the slave master, "she insisted… She is not one to be denied, I assure you."

"Insisted? How the hell can she insist on anything? She has no face! And you are not one to assure me of anything!" Forkav let his frustration get the better of him as he exclaimed with a booming voice, deeper and grittier than it normally was, "I am aware of her success in the junker arenas. But it only gave her foolish hope. I am Elder Junker—I am the king's Left Hand! There is no one more skilled in hand-to-hand combat than I! You have brought this girl to her death!" He spat on the slowly freezing mud.

"Defend your King and get this over with." Goranth Brokenshaft, the Right Hand of the king, commanded.

Forkav let out an exaggerated sigh and resumed his glare at the slave master.

"You old fool, I will shred your back with live jumper

wire when this is over. Because of you, I will have yet another child's death to haunt my dreams. Turn on the damn light."

The slave master scurried over to an old iron sconce mounted on the pit's timber wall. He nearly dropped the battery and steel wool as he struggled to the light it with trembling hands. The flames caught, and he shoved it in the oil-soaked light fixture. He then scurried out of the pit like frightened vermin.

Forkav sighed again as he unbuckled the straps of his iron breastplate, made from an old tank's hull access plate. His squire ran off with the Forkav's greatsword and hastily returned to carry away the breastplate.

Nyala's skin morphed into something translucent. Red blush became visible through the thin flesh, and her veins darkened. Her heart thumped wildly, and her breathing hastened. Only a roughly spun linen cloth covered her chest and loins for modesty. She wore nothing else but bumps on her smoky-clear skin, in reaction to the brisk air that rolled off the frozen mountains and into the valley where the barbaric capital village was established.

Forkav bore his thick chest and considerable musculature as he struggled to hide his shock at Nyala, who was exposing terrifying features not of a human. He stripped down to his own loincloth but struggled to remove his leggings.

Nyala charged towards the man as fast as she could. He ripped off the leggings and tossed them aside. She dropped and slid between his legs. He countered the surprise and grabbed her by the shoulder. She curled up and kicked him in the lower back, causing him to stumble forward and lose his grip. She charged again, but he spun around quick enough to knock her back with his massive arm. He charged at her.

She slapped and blocked every advance as he struggled to grab a hold of her. He grunted in frustration. They continued the dance for a while, both waiting for the other to make a mistake. Forkav did first. He nearly rolled his ankle, and she dived at his knee, shattering it in the process.

He uncomfortably got his feet with a hop, but no other sign of expressed pain. She was painfully aware that everyone here was tough. Too tough. Sensitive emotions were rarely shown. She charged with a vicious attack of punches, kicks, and shoves. Forkav failed every attempt to stand. She stomped on his broken knee repeatedly. He clenched his teeth but released no other sign of weakness and managed to dig his fingernails deep into her shoulder.

She gripped his beard braid firmly and hammered his face with her other fist until his own blood covered it entirely. His defences weakened, and he could scarcely lift his arms. She dug her fingernails into his throat.

She pressed until the skin tore. She buried her fingers deep inside his flesh and wrapped them around his larynx, trachea, thyroid, and everything else in there, ensuring a firm grip, despite the heavily flowing blood. She leaned on Forkav's face to brace her strength and ripped the man's throat out. The upper spine behind the throat snapped from the tug. His body shook violently, but lifelessly.

She stood up straight and seemed to gaze at the falling moon. She flung the gore in the direction of the rising sun and then faced the right hand of the king. Goranth kept his expression strong and determined. He ripped off his armour one piece at a time as he cursed irreverently.

Forkav's squire sprinted over to Nyala as if charging. Goranth simply shook his head as he continued stripping off his armour. She braced herself for an attack but could not understand the boy's concerned rather than angered expression. He dropped to his knees and wiped away blood from a scrape on her knee. The skin in that area flushed white and seemed to stiffen a bit, like goose flesh. She pulled away from him. He seemed confused for a heartbeat and moved to clean the gashes on her shoulder.

"He's your squire now, foolish bitch."

Goranth approached in nothing but his loincloth. He sucked up snot into his throat and spat on the ground. His own skinned tightened like that of a goose in brisk cold air.

"You don't know that because you've never killed a Kul before. Because you only hold thirteen years! You are skilled enough in combat to look for mistakes, and to capitalise on those mistakes, to defeat your opponent. But you will not survive against an opponent that makes no mistakes."

Goranth ripped off his loincloth and flexed entirely nude. "And I'm going to kill you with my balls out and my bludgeon swinging. Fear does not reside here."

Nyala kept her distance this time as they circled each

other. Goranth lunged for her a few times, but she deflected his arms. He lost patience and charged. She was caught off guard, not expecting the man to make an amateur move. Amateur for him. The large brutish men were quite vain and avoided any movements or tactics that would encourage the appearance of weakness or desperation.

He successfully wrapped his arms around her like a bear and squeezed her slender frame with all his might. She struggled to free her arms, but his embrace was too fierce to defy. A crack from somewhere inside her rose concern, but no pain followed.

She squirmed and twisted as best as she could, but could not break free. She hoped to outlast his energy, but he did not seem to be tiring, and he was an impressively strong man. Clouds flooded the fringes of her vision and drowsiness crept into her mind. She realised her imminent loss.

She fumbled his manhood with her feet, trying desperately to pinch, squeeze, or hurt him, but could just not seem to get a grip. More cracks and crunches warmed her chest with panic. She could not find comfort anywhere in the energy around her. A tingling spread across her chest and filled her sight with bright light.

Then, what she imagined to be pain shot down her neck and spine. Every muscle in her body seemed to lose strength. She felt blood. It trickled down her thigh. The strangest light came to her. She felt something, for the first time, in her face. Exactly where she knows other humans to have their eyes. And there was light outside of her face skin. She knew what humans looked like from the energy they emit, but this, this was different. She could see a rough silhouette of the man squeezing the life out of her.

The blood was hot. It continued to spill down her thighs, and it came from inside of her. Her crotch ached, and cramps brought her more pain than this brute. Then she felt something open on her face and felt suddenly compelled to free herself from her face skin. To breathe. To suck in air.

Goranth watched the horrific shapes move inside of Nyala's face but kept his grip tight. When she emitted the most peculiar and terrifyingly eerie sound, he slacked a bit. She swiftly slipped her knees up in between their chests and shoved off. Goranth stumbled backward and tripped over Forkav's bloody corpse.

Nyala got to her feet and drove her fingertips into the face skin covering her mouth and tore it open, shoving aside the excruciating pain it caused. The cold air bit her teeth and lips, and she sucked in her first breath as deep as she could. The sound the inhale made tickled her throat and triggered a fit of coughing in between breaths.

Goranth, the king, and everyone else watched in utter bewilderment as the infamous faceless girl grew one right before their eyes. An arrow, swifter than a bolt of lightning, zipped through the freezing air and stopped halfway through Nyala's chest. She gasped like a leprous woman who has smoked all her life. Then she wailed. The sound was abnormally loud and sent shivers up everyone's spines.

She collapsed onto the oily mud that was hardening in the cold air. No one moved aside from turning to look upon the king, who had cheated the laws of honour by using his compound bow, robbing her of the chance of a fair challenge.

"That…isn't human…doesn't count."

The squire scurried as everyone else watched him in bafflement. He hastened over to a toolshed and frantically grabbed different gadgets and gizmos. He shouted at the sponsor, "Grab her soul magnets!"

"Th-the ones attuned to her?" he stuttered.

"Yes, of course the ones attuned to her! Snap out of it, man, quick! It is in her pack!"

The squire dragged over a heavy machine that was permanently fastened to a hand dolly, though its wheels were flat, and one of them shattered. The boy muscled through the resistant mud as he dragged the rusted equipment over to Nyala's body.

He uncoiled what looked like massive jumper cables and clamped them on her. The clamps were snap traps at one point, intended for bears. The squire snapped one on each foot. The sponsor jogged over with a massive wiring harness and set it on her head. He pulled a leather strap underneath her chin and buckled it to the other side.

The boy pulled on some levers and turned some dials. Then he rubbed to defibrillator pads together to create static electricity and placed them on Nyala's chest.

"Don't do it, kid," Goranth muttered.

The boy ran over to Forkav's clothes and rummaged

through them as the sponsor held the pads on her chest. The machine emitted an electrical whirring sound that grew in volume. The boy pulled out a gemstone from Forkav's clothes and held it up in the air, allowing the brightness of the fully awake sun to shine through it. Something inside the gem seems to move, like water trapped under the ice of a frozen lake. He hustled back to Nyala.

"Is that?" The sponsor asked.

"It is." The boy pressed the gem into a spot built for it inside the machine. Nyala lay lifeless with a bloody mouth exposed through torn face skin.

"Wait," the sponsor said as he tore the rest of the face skin away from her newly formed nose and eyes. Everyone was stunned but silent. The sponsor returned to the defibrillator pads and nodded at the squire. The boy pressed a momentary push button, and a flash of white forced everyone to squint.

The light returned to normal, and the machine sputtered to silent stillness. Water trickled far off in the distance. Breeze played with the brush. The sun hid behind freezing clouds. The cold kept everyone alert. And Nyala opened her eyes.

VAMPIRE WORLD

R.S. Nevil

"Look what we have here…"

Panic shook Garva as he turned, his reward slipping from his grasp.

"It seems one of the humans has escaped from the farm."

The voice rang out into the night, orange eyes peering back at him through the darkness. Garva knew what they were. The scent of blood had given them away.

"It's been a long time since we've seen a rogue human," the vampire said.

"How right you are, Cristobal. It makes me miss the old days, back when we still had to hunt for our food."

Back before the vampires had taken over.

A DOSE OF NO CLOSURE

Barend Nieuwstraten III

Atop the stairs to the dining hall, the assassin revelled in the wake of his task's completion. He'd waited long enough for the merriment to cease echoing down the stairs to the kitchen.

A fatally tainted feast where all attendees were slumped lifeless. Thwarted mid-gluttony, there was no sound but the crackling of the hearth. That was until a burp drew the killer's attention. One guest remained, still eating and drinking, raising a crossbow from under the table.

"There is an explanation," he said, as a bolt entered the assassin's eye. "But you've no longer the time to hear it."

THE TIME OF THE NIGHT-WACCHE

John Lane

King Chaucer Frederick, in full combat garb, entered through the screen passage in order to get to the Great Hall of Cold Comfort Castle, his personal residence and fortification against the Night-wacche. Held by the straps in his left hand was a shield decorated with a painted black dragon, the crest of the House of Frederick. In his right held a broadsword, its leather covered handle also ornamented with the black dragon crest. King Frederick kept shifting his focus from one side of the room to another, watching for anyone not belonging in the Hall. The king trusted no one with his gear ever since on the day of succession when supposedly one of the servants sold his garments to members of the Night-wacche for several gold coins. He never found out who. He never trusted another servant after that.

While every part of his body throbbed from dull pain, King Chaucer Frederick took each step very slow, the sound of boots echoing throughout the room. His white and red cross surcoat carried several dark red stains. Also smeared in red was a cloth bag tied with rope that attached to his belt.

Hung from the chandelier were several lighted tallow candles that gave off enough brightness so that the king could navigate his way through the room.

The king passed by the large bay window on his side of the Hall. An intrusive thought interrupted the quiet in his brain. He wondered what would happen if one of the peasants were to get a glimpse of him through the window. Would they react more to a seemingly battle-weary knight or to the teenaged boy that just led his first campaign against the Night-wacche? He struggled to shut his mind off at such nonsense.

The warmth against his cold cheeks made for a good distraction. At the far end was a lit fireplace, where smoke rose until it vented through an opening in the ceiling. Someone took the foresight to start the fire. In a rare show of gratitude, he was very thankful since he caught a chill easily from living in the drafty castle all his life.

Another sight pleased him. At his seat, nearest to the fireplace, was a plate full of smoked ham and bread. His stomach grumbled. Without the luxury of the previous evening's food or drink, he'd fasted before fighting in the late morning campaign. A successful one by his standards, whereby he killed thirteen of the Night-wacche on Bard's Hill, miles away, and cut their hands off for trophies.

He sensed something in control throughout the battle. Something unable to be explained.

He arrived at his place at the table, but another matter troubled his mind.

Bard's Hill. The supposed high ground that the Night-wacche planned to use as a rallying point to attack the castle, or so he thought. *Wait*— There were places with more valuable real estate to conquer, and at a more strategic location than Bard's Hill. Knight's Hill sloped right into the keep. Devil's Mountain contained a passageway that linked with the entrance to the castle's dungeon. If true, then why Bard's Hill? This bothered the king. Two days ago, a female servant intercepted a message on parchment from the Night-wacche, threatening an attack the next day. But how did she get the message? He never bothered to ask, because he saw this as an opportunity for victory at any cost. Victory to make a name for himself. Then, exactly two dozen men in combat gear on horseback waited for him at the front of the castle. Before Chaucer became king, these men believed that he would make for an incompetent ruler. Then, at the Hill, the men came across fifty members of the Night-wacche, unarmed and unclothed, save for tunics. There was no encampment, nothing to suggest they stayed there for any length of time. They went down easily, like churned butter. He had no problem slaying his share and collecting mementos. It all came together so easily. Maybe much too easily. Maybe this was nothing more than another intrusive thought to challenge his own fitness as a leader? Either way, he needed another distraction.

The king pulled out the wooden ornamental chair, the one with the black dragon carved on all sides, then flopped on the seat. The king removed his metal helmet and his chain mail gauntlets and placed them on the chair within arm's reach. He set the shield against the table, then loosened the rope around the bag, enough to separate it from his clothing. It was dropped to the floor.

Chaucer knew one thing. He needed a drink. Now.

He lifted the mug, put it to his lips, but nothing emerged. He looked inside at eye level. Still, nothing. Doesn't the king have the right to have his thirst quenched? The longer he stared at its empty state, the more he gritted his teeth.

"Sider!" Chaucer remembered being told the story of Thomas the Carking by an older servant. On a particular day, long ago, when the sun was at its highest point in the heavens, Thomas refused to bring the king his requested beverage. Chaucer never learned the name of who it said, but it did not matter. Thomas—that one particular male servant—reasoned that it was his job to decide how much the king is allowed to drink since he "walken abouten." After calling Thomas's name several times, and armed with broadsword in hand, the king found and cornered the "thinkere" in the smokehouse. One swipe later, and the king turned the male servant into a eunuch, a slow death from blood that emptied from his testicleless body. Then, during the next light of day, four knights strung the servant up by the arms on a pole positioned on the other side of the moat. The king used it as a warning for not recognising him as ultimate authority. Chaucer smiled.

A wench carried a rounded jug with both hands. She motioned for the cup, and he slid it over to her side of the table. She poured the caramel-coloured liquid until it reached the rim. He tasted the drink. Much too sweet. More than usual, as if crushed berries and apples were mixed together. Interesting. That was the last complaint of his father and brother after their last drink. The last complaint before they each entered a never-ending sleep. He never felt any sorrow for their passing. Father was constantly cold towards him, blaming the boy for everything from the loss of a battle to something as minor as his stew being served cold, all while his brother stood by, never wanting another sibling to compete with for the throne.

The wench looked him up and down. "*Bataille*?"

"*Ya. Killen flok.*" He picked up the bag from the floor and dumped the contents onto the table. Thirteen pairs of shrivelled skeletal hands. Each one consisted of three bony fingers and thumb.

She swallowed hard at the sight of the malformed hands. "Night-wacche?"

The king smiled. "Ya."

"Bataille ethy?"

He patted one of the hands. "*Verrei.*"

Out of the corner of his eye, the king saw her nod towards the far corner of the room. He thought he heard something, like the sliding of a cloak across the floor, but he looked around and did not see anything. For a moment, he thought his shadow shifted, but he wondered if he imagined the whole thing. He still did not like sudden movements from his servants. They might be hiding something.

As she walked away, the king grabbed her by the arm. The wench said, "*Ei!*" She lost control of the jug. The vessel fell with a clang and the entire contents of cider spilled all over the floor. He stared into her eyes and jerked his head up and down several times. "*Hwy nodden?*"

"*Ic no nodden.*" Her body shook. Small beads of sweat appeared on her forehead.

"Yau nodden."

She tried to pull away, but the king tightened his grip. "*No nodden.*"

Chaucer pulled her closer. He grabbed the broadsword by the handle. "*Yau liere.*"

"No nodden. NO NODDEN!"

Chaucer thrusted the sword through her stomach until the point came through her back. Her dress covered with blood, she spat drops of crimson from her mouth. He pulled the sword out and her body fell to the ground.

While she screamed, "*Helpe*," the king took large bites of ham and bread, and drank cider, as if nothing happened.

And then, as if karma punished him, a series of incidents happened simultaneously.

Every time he tried to pick up some food off his plate, he struggled to hold it in his hands. He felt his heart try to jump out of his chest. He saw two images of the table, one on top of the other. The light from the candles started to hurt his eyes, but the king could not lift himself out of his chair. Somehow, he did not make himself aware that the fire died out. And the worst of it, his mouth turned dry and his throat was parched.

He grabbed the mug, but his inability to hold anything caused the mug to fall to the floor. The liquid quickly dumped out.

Then his shadow moved again. Silhouettes from the candles also moved. They grew, split in half, grew, split in half. The cycle continued, uninterrupted, until the room was surrounded by individual shadows. All at once, each shadow removed its cloak to reveal thousands of skeletal faces, each one with shimmering bodies and eye sockets that glowed white in the near darkness.

The king recognised them immediately. The Night-wacche.

The entities surrounded him until they took every inch of space around him. The king's eyes started to droop.

The leader—the one with eye sockets that glowed the brightest—spoke. "You don't understand my speech because we come from the far future."

The king now struggled to keep his eyes open. His throat was so parched, he could barely get the words out. "*Hou? Hou art thee?*"

"You can't comprehend, so don't try. Before we take your life, and to soothe our own conscience, I want to at least share with you why we feel justified to cause your existence to cease."

"*Hou? Hou art thee?*" The king's eyes were completely shut, his head lay on the table.

"You don't even grasp what I told you, so don't bother to speak. Yes, we poisoned your father, your brother, and now you. Your children, many generations down the road, will be responsible for wiping out most of our species. All because your species' greed consumed you to invade our planet and take over our resources, since your species ended up depleting your own resources—polluting your rivers and streams. Depleting the ozone layer by carbon emissions. Destroying your planet with fracking. You think you can do it to our planet.

"Yes, we fought with rocks and sticks, but your species overpowered ours with laser guns, bone-eating missiles, tanks and what not. Your takeover of our planet was complete within a few days."

The king snored.

"A few of us had the foresight to escape. We fled to a neighbouring star system. Over the next hundreds of years, we developed our own technology, including the secret of time travel. We learned that your president was Steven Johnson, and we were able to trace his ancestry to the three of you. Killing you all, we can stop the madness that your species infected on ours. Your father is dead. Your brother is dead. And now you."

Several members of the Night-wacche held him down. The king offered no resistance. The leader picked up the king's broadsword.

"Yes, we sacrificed some of our men by the end of your sword, but that was the only way to get you out of the castle—to plant this idea of a battle in your head. I won't disclose to you how we did it, but we convinced a few knights, the wench, the right people, to carry out our plan. The rest of us who survived had to wait until you left so we could be in the proper position, so that we could all see your demise when the time was right.

"Yes, the wench did nod to signal to us her part in our plan was completed. We knew it would not be long before your end.

"We allowed your father and brother to die in peace, but you... You are different. And our species saved the best for you. The few of our scientists that lived predicted your future offspring will lead the actual attack. We are here to collect our trophy, just as you did."

The leader raised the sword, then slammed it down with such a force it sliced through his neck in one swing, decapitating his head from the rest of his body.

Judgement

Vijayaraj Mahendraraj

He begged, "We've only ever served the crown, sire. My Ana cared for your children for—"

"Long enough! Her services are no longer needed. As are yours, executioner. Sometimes, judgement comes by way of rags in the streets," the king interjected, beneath a crown of bone.

They were escorted out, shamed and shunned. Her knowledge of the castle granted them entry that night. It took little cunning to line their drinks with sedating nightshade and little strength for the enormous axe to perform its bidding. One by one, judgement came by way of crimson sheets in the royal house.

ADVANCE OF THE GRIMSAILS

Jasiah Witkofsky

When the corvette, *A Picada Rapida*, was beset upon by the corsair, *La Voile Sinistre*—the GrimSails—the unexpected happened when the bombarded defenders boarded the attackers who had drawn alongside the Portuguese ship transporting the Purple Pistollera and a handful of the Crimson Cinquedea gang up towards the French coastline. In a manner most unusual, a number of the said passengers aboard the assaulted vessel were the first to lead the charge.

Amongst the initial wave to swing the ropes towards the piratical aggressors was the swift Pistollera, followed closely by Jerome the Moor. When others followed suit, chaos ensued.

Unleashing her firearm from a violet-striped sash and

cocking the dog lock, the Pistollera sent an explosive shot into the sky, slicing through the rope being used by a shirtless seadog to launch himself at their vessel, and disrupting his swooping trajectory to come crashing down into the waves. With well-practiced manoeuvres, Jerome dashed forth with his broad-bladed sabre to guard her back from any close quarters attacks as she expertly reloaded her pistol. A cadre of their companions in arms zipped past the duo to engage in the fray.

Taken by surprise at the bold advance of the defenders, the buccaneers lost some ground upon their own vessel, backpedalling from the exuberant rush off the Portuguese corvette. But this momentary retreat held its ground upon realising they outnumbered the boarders more than two to one. The clanging of rapier, cutlass, stiletto, and the occasional blast of black powder, rang from fore to stern.

Dolores, the Pistollera, noticed a trio of scallywags wheel forth a cast-bronze cannon to deliver a catastrophic point-blank shot at the Portuguese vessel. Tugging on Jerome's billowing sleeve, now flecked with the blood of his enemies, she directed the swordsman to the cannoneers.

With the hardwood butt of her custom-crafted musket, she smashed the hand of the man reaching into a crate of steel-grey cannonballs as Jerome sliced deep into the forearm of the man holding the fusee, before shouldering the third over the rails into the ocean blue. For her efforts, the cannon-loader backhanded Dolores with his uninjured fist. Seeing this, Jerome turned with a snarl and drove his curved death-dealer straight through the offender's sternum, locking eyes with the man as blood spewed from the corners of his mouth.

Dolores turned away from the gruesome sight. "Before you revel in your bloodlust, Jerome, know that our comrades are in dire need of our assistance."

The battle-charged man followed the diminutive female into the midship melee, yelling his hoarse shout at the top of his lungs, his frazzled beard flecked with foam and fury. Their fellow guardians and guerrillas fared well enough aboard the enemy's corsair. Despite the numbers being against them, they were retaining turf advantage claimed by the sea-bandits, who knew every nook and cranny of their sleek ocean-treader. More than a couple of fighters from both sides groaned and bled out upon the wooden planks of the weathered deck, worn smooth by the boot stomps, time, and the elements.

Dolores slowed her advance and stashed her pistol to aid one of the fallen, just as Jerome dashed by in a mad dance of savagery, tempered only by an ingrained devotion to the art of the sword. His back-and-forth slashes from a blade wider than a sabre, yet slimmer than a scimitar, carved an arc that helped even the odds between combatants.

Meanwhile, Dolores cradled the head of Giuseppe DaParma upon her lap on the fringe of the skirmish as he breathed his last.

"Dearest Giuseppe, you have been such a boon upon our escapades. Both large and small, high and low…your voice has heralded the way for our coming and smoothed the transitions of that which would have been an otherwise rocky path." She slicked back his sweat-dampened hair with gentle caresses.

"Oh, pretty Pistollera. Jerome was right. It was all worth it, for your sake and your cause. Never let any soul doubt your fervour and rectitude." The wordsmith broke off to begin a new tangent. "Sweet Dolores, do you remember the time we tussled beneath the—"

Dolores cut him off with a curt finger to his lips. "Of course, my Giuseppe. I shall never forget. Though a single night, still your tenderness and shy passion reverberates throughout my mind. Never shall I discard or disregard that evening of bliss we shared of oneness..."

She did not need to lower his eyelids over those bewitching blues, for he shuttered them closed ever so gently while nestled on her lap, sighing one final breath.

It was at this moment of heartbreak and cacophony that the captain of the GrimSails made his entrance from his private quarters, intimidating all with his swagger and undeniable presence. At the ascendant deck from which he emerged, the belligerent figure stood resplendent in his burgundy thigh-high boots of polished leather, overlapping pantaloons of the light grey variety. His shale knee-length overcoat, bedecked with a double layer of whalebone buttons, provided a stylish exterior. It swathed the loose cream-coloured shirt, cinched with a charcoal-tinted cummerbund that housed his trusted ***épée***and coiled whipcord beneath a studded belt of cured rawhide. Below a tattered yet full hat, decorated with ostrich and peacock feathers, a black mask surrounded his pale blue eyes—one lighter than the other. Below that sprouted an unkempt beard of grey-blonde bristles, unshorn for moons…a sure sign of defiance, defamation, or both—the notorious Grey Grim Jivan.

"Ahoy and gangway, ye lily-livered lubbers! When ye cross me waters, ye cross me!" the crazed tyrant roared. "All who sail the briny, pay the tithe! So claims I!" The unhinged villain launched a double brace of musketry into the heavens, enunciating his declaration with brimstone finality. "Mateys! Do not allow this wench and her fops to tread upon your spineless carcasses. Attack!"

Dropping a spent musket, he unravelled his whip and lashed out the eye of the nearest to him—friend or foe, he cared not. The audacious captain waltzed down the short flight of stairs into the battle as if entering a ballroom dance as the guest of honour, his demented cackle piercing the crescendo of combat.

Steel sang sharp falsettos against steel—and sometimes low and baritone into flesh and marrow—as the contestants pitted their lives against each other. At one end, Jerome cleaving a crimson trail for his cohorts to rally behind at the driving march of an allegro, while the Grim capitaine sauntered a gay dolce, lashing his way through the miasma of bodies, as nonchalant as a bored orchestral conductor, sweeping through men as if they were misplaced notes in a syncopated masterpiece. Both capitaine and Cinquedea never missing a beat in their respective time signatures.

The Pistollera, blinking back tears with her long dark lashes, eased Giuseppe's head upon the deck to once more draw her short-barrel and take her part, yet again, amongst the ruckus. Firing another lead ball above the heads of the embattled, Dolores shattered a picaroon's notched blade in half, allowing a Genoese mercenary to plunge his foil into the bowels of the disarmed raider. The tangle of warriors had become so intertwined at this point it was impossible to determine which side held the closer claim to victory.

The nearness of the duelling ships began to create a precarious swelling of waves betwixt the two hulls, which would soon lead to a collision that could undoubtedly send both vessels to the bottom of the Atlantic. The crew who retained their posts guiding the *Picada Rapida* began shouting for the assistance of their men aboard the GrimSails, whose sailors threw out their own desperate cries of warning about the dire circumstances.

Hesitantly at first, the fighting men began to take heed of the calls of their mates and, with trepidation, retreated from their fatal engagements. The flight from combat picked up momentum on both sides—men willing to die upon the blade or by musket fire, scrambled in fear to avoid plunging beneath the murky depths to the monstrous horrors that lurked below. A handful of soldiers from the Portuguese corvette managed to brutishly offload one of the deadly two-ton cannons overboard, before scurrying to the ropes to swing back to friendly company. Shouts came from the *Picada,* directed at any stragglers remaining aboard the pirate ship, as they began unmooring the cables connecting the two flotillas.

Dolores heard the calls of her companions who had escaped from the enemy's boat as she finished powder tamping her gun, but she would not depart hostile territory without Jerome. The sabre-wielding dervish now had a clear view of the Grim capitaine, whose whip lashed about like the flailing tentacle of an octopus. The masked and bearded overseer of the pillagers aimed his pistol at the Cinquedea's chest and misfired. Cursing the unreliable weapon, he tossed it aside to face his opponent, hand to hand. Jerome skipped forwards to narrow the distance between him and the head of the beast, allowing his cleaver a biting edge. Despite his fancy footwork and erratic movements, the capitaine's estimations proved accurate, as he let loose a lightning crack from his long leather braid to savagely slap across his opponent's face, halting Jerome in his tracks, and leaving a bloody trail across his already seamed features.

Taking full advantage of the blinding diversion, the pirate lord sashayed forwards, looping his flexible sidearm about the Tuscan's neck. Regardless of Jerome's veteran status, the dreaded capitaine held an indisputable advantage over his smaller, surly opponent. Sidestepping around the lashed man to stand at his rear, he wound Jerome's throat tightly with several swift loops of his lariat while prying the curved blade from his foe's grip. Booting his captive thrice in the kidneys, the strangler forced the air-deprived swordsman to the edge of the ship. Hitching the whip's handle to the rail, the Grim capitaine kicked the suffocating man overboard to dangle like a hooked fish. Turning, Grey Jivan drew his thin sword from its battered sheath with a maniacal grin.

Kkr-BANG!

The ornate-hilted epee was blown from the capitaine's stunned and paralysed grasp by a lead shot embedded squarely in the centre of the weapon's handle. The Purple Pistollera stood poised before the astonished pirate with gun smoke seeping from the barrel's opening, misting her exquisite features in a drifting haze of sulphur and magnesium.

"You shall allow both me and my keelhauled compatriot to remove ourselves from your ill fortuned transport, and we will both go about our merry ways with no further harm to either party. Is that understood?" She held aloft a thin dagger within her offhand for emphasis, daring the buccaneer to challenge her request.

"Your shot is spent, *Mademoiselle*," retorted the capitaine with a bow. "What makes you believe I would not saunter over to your ravishing side and have my way with you in any way I see fit?" the man goaded between a jaundiced leer.

"Dolores arced her weighted dagger to give heightened forbearance to her words. "Do not tempt me, fiend. As you have witnessed, I have disarmed you with a shot few, if any, could perform. Do you doubt my precision with the knife as well? The choice is yours, but I advise caution and rationale upon your decision making. For it is thee who lies weaponless and at the mercy of my temperament, which lies stressed and pulled to a hair's trigger."

Meanwhile, as Grim Jivan pondered his predicament and the veracity of the Pistollera's claim, Jerome had managed to kick off his riding boots as he swung by the neck above the choppy waters of the deep blue. Using the tight crevices of the steam-curled wooden boards that held the vessel afloat and watertight, he toed his way to some semblance of freedom from the bonds that shackled his airway. Amidst the cheers of his loyal crewmates, he scoured his way loose of the sinuous bindings that girded his neck with the freshly procured Toledo dagger. With a gusty heave that pitched his body back aboard the enemy corsair, Jerome tumbled to his discarded sabre, kneeling defensively behind the pirate with wheezing and hacking breaths.

"I shall not repeat myself!" Dolores held firm in her convictions, confidence boosted by the reappearance of her friend.

Extracting a fuse from his studded belt, Grim Jivan skirted over to the last of the readied cannons, daring to play his ace in the hole. "A single move from either one of you and I shall send your rickety bundle of saturated driftwood and tattered sails to the bowels of Hell!"

"Then my fine edge takes your head, and we take command of your vessel." Jerome spat out his threat from a ravaged throat.

The greybeard mulled over his prospects before

flicking the smoking charge into the ocean. "Stand by then, you mongrels! I shall scuttle your wee boaty another day. On this ye have me promise."

The Pistollera and Jerome edged away carefully, backpedalling towards the loose riggings that would carry them to safety. The pirates jeered and spat at the retreating duo as they grasped firm to their ropes.

"Have you caught wind enough to cross, Jerome?" Dolores asked, concern lacing her lowered voice.

"As ready as I'll ever be, *ragazza*," the swordsman croaked.

With gallant lunges, the Catalonian beauty and the ugly Tuscan, sword still drawn, dashed from the corsair to the corvette with the backdrop of crows hooted by their mates, and the curses cried out from their foes. With quick flicks of the wrist, Jerome severed the last ties binding the vessels together by little more than a fathom. The steersmen expertly cranked their wheels to create distance without scraping hulls or colliding rudders.

The sails and currents pulled the clashing sailors further and further away from each other, until individual silhouettes could no longer be perceived from either deck. Cannon shot was launched from the blood-soaked planks of the GrimSails, but the echoing explosion landed far off course from the *Picada Rapida*——no attack, for the projected missile landed far from their location. More likely a salute and a send-off for a noteworthy opponent.

Dolores dropped from her perch upon the side rails to pirouette and address Jerome. "Are you doing well, my friend? That is quite the nasty weal across your nose."

"Bah. What's one more scar, *ragazza*?" The brooding figure winced as he tried to adjust his facial features. "But how is your eye? Looks like you went a little heavy on the makeup asymmetrically, if I dare say."

Dolores cupped her right eye—the adrenaline had run so high she didn't even notice the bruising that now swelled her lovely face.

"Yes, yes… I guess we both shall survive this surprise attack." Then Dolores began to come to terms with the greater reality of the circumstances. "Yet others have not. Poor Giuseppe, and others, and others that did not survive the encounter."

"Aye, *ragazza*," Jerome conceded the news of the loss. "He had a big mouth...but a bigger heart. The Cinquedeas have taken an arterial blow that can never be truly healed. We shall celebrate his words and deeds when we have completed our journey home." He pulled off his red bandanna to wave the headcloth in tandem with the sea breeze, as custom decreed. A subcultural gesture to the dearly departed.

Turning back to the Pistollera, Jerome noticed her gnawing on the side of her lip. Knowing this look of internal deliberation, he pried into her with his sunken gaze. "What burdens your mind, *ragazza*? We suffered some losses, tis true, but we managed to storm the enemy and humiliate the mighty GrimSails…we can't expect a much better result than that."

Dolores tilted her head and seemed to look through her

faithful sidekick. "I can't get this notion out of my head that I have met this Capitaine Jivan before. If only I could have seen his face without the mask. I swear…his laugh was so hauntingly familiar…" Her voice trailed off as she racked her brain for any memory connected with her recent seafaring encounter.

Jerome cocked a jutting eyebrow at the dainty heroine. "One of your many lovers, mayhaps? Perhaps that craven deserter you were so intent on marrying? Hhmmm…"

Dolores kicked at Jerome's shins for his taunting jibes as he snickered, dancing away from her pointed boots. His humour was brash, personal, and ham-fisted, but he knew it got the job done when he saw her eyes glitter and the fine, upward twist of the corners of her mouth. The heaviness of the mood further lightened when the man in the crow's nest shouted his sighting of a Basque port town at the crook between Spain and France.

The mass of boatmen, wounded and hale alike, cheered the heralding of fortunate news as the finest keg of hops-brew was rolled foredecks for all to partake in celebratory fashion—their voyage was nearing completion, a great boon for those who had never sailed the frothing expanse and had spent every moment in quaking anxiety. Foaming inebriation poured down salt-parched throats, jigs were initiated, and ribald songs of shamelessness and valour rang through the open air.

Though Dolores typically found ale to be a wretched beverage, she partook with the menfolk, and the lukewarm intoxicant did make her battered eye feel better. The

Picada Rapida hugged the coastline tight, refusing to lose sight of the brink as they drifted ever closer to St Nazaire to offload the Genoese entourage, more than ready to stretch their legs upon solid ground.

The revelry dissipated Dolores's gloomy mindset, and Jerome managed to pull her into a dance to the raucous amusement of crew and passengers alike. Spinning in place to the claps and stomps of the mariners, she broke off from her twirling to heft a solid gulp of amber ale before addressing the men she had boarded with for several weeks.

"The way to the Bourbon Empire lies clear, my merry fellows! And if not…we have proven we shall wipe the path clean of the peril of any who dare obstruct us!"

The shipmen burst into roars of applause, drawing their blades and clanging the swords together in self-satisfied jubilation. The shouts of celebration were so loud they reached the ears of other boaters, who waved them on in the spirit of camaraderie. Floating upon calm and friendly waters, the revellers upon the *Picada* drank and danced their woes and wounds to the wind.

THE INVITED AND THE UNINVITED

Barend Nieuwstraten III

Five skulls upon an altar wore wigs of melted wax within a circle. The ranger wondered what he'd found as the scent of sulphur stung his nostrils. No sign of the man he'd followed for days within this remote cabin that creaked in the slightest breeze.

It was the gentle red drizzle, precipitating indoors, that soon drew his eyes to the ceiling. Enough viscera to build a man was violently spread upon it. Only then did the ranger notice the breathing. Two burning amber eyes in a shadowed corner looking back.

A moment of agony. Then there was silent darkness.

WANTED

Blen

It's funny how we were the evil ones when humans were the ones who were so intimidated by our power that they killed us for it. Most witches and wizards concealed their powers and lived among humans, but my face was all over the wanted posters with an order to kill on sight.

I had no choice but to resort to dark magic. I'm not proud of how many people I've killed. But I haven't done anything wrong, not really.

My only crime was being born when witches and wizards were deemed evil, and so burned alive because of it.

MERCY

L.J. McLeod

So it came to this. Queen against king. Wife against husband. He raised his hand against her. She raised her army against him. Now she faced him once more, already coated by the gore of battle. Spattered with blood, he smirked at her.

"Are you done with your tantrum, my love?"

She lunged; their swords clashed. Violence shone from his eyes.

Never again.

She hooked his foot, bringing him to his knees. Her sword pressed to his throat.

"Mercy," he begged.

She pushed her sword deeper, spilling blood. Mercy was for the weak—she would never be weak again.

MOTE

A. Lily

It's difficult for Paul to recall when this ritual began. There was a vague remembrance of it having been around, or on, the day of the thirtieth anniversary of when *she* was gone. At least, on the day he *realised* she was gone. There wasn't much he remembered now. Not her name. Not even his own, and this is a startling realisation for him. How much longer until he forgot all that lay outside his property line, and what resided in the woods beyond? Secretly, he hoped that day would come soon. But he guards this thought against the rustle in the bush, as what's offered is dragged, screeching through the hedge.

Rising to his feet, he took the last swill of something bitter in his cup and held it momentarily on his tongue before exhaling fumes that linger, suspended in the night air, long after the screen door closes behind him.

* * *

Things make sense in the morning. There's a chair near the door, facing the foot of his bed and, while digging out a pair of jeans from the laundry basket, he sees that the dust is lightly brushed within a faint shape on its seat. There's an outline swirling in the luminescence of airborne debris, suspended in the rising sunlight.

It's hardly there. It'll be gone by the time the sun's fallen below the horizon of trees. He knows that with a certainty stronger than the pressure his expanded bladder gave him. Until then, he'll piss and go to work in his neighbour's garden. Maybe tonight will be different.

* * *

"Cats are disappearing."

"Cats?"

"Ya" Jonas pauses and puts down the shovel. He glances at Paul, then averts his eyes. Is he scared? *He should be*, Paul thinks to himself with a sadness he hadn't expected to feel. He continues to push freshly turned earth.

"They say, uh...you might have something to do with it."

"Really? What makes them say that?"

"While hunting, Gene found bones along your property line. Little ones, carved up like ornaments. He brought some to show me. I know you used to carve wood—damn good at it, from what I remember. Looked a lot like what you used to make."

This was a surprise to him. *Carved like ornaments.*

The thought repeats itself in Paul's mind all day, pounding like a drumbeat.

* * *

Whatever hid in those woods had a hunger. In the beginning, he remembered its mewling shadow flitting through the trees and into the bushes. It began with leftovers; some chicken bones. And as it grew, so did its appetite. The better able he was to satiate it, the closer he was to realising the mirage of light and colour on the chair was actually *her*.

Lost in his mind, he comes across an idea and plans to execute it. It was horrible to consider, but then again, at this point, he was desperate enough to try anything.

Anything to bring her back.

* * *

The screams were the worst he had ever heard that night. He was grateful for the expanse of field between his and Jonas' home. No doubt the man had heard something, but then again, why should he care? He was beyond that point now. But, God damn it, he was getting closer. He could feel it as the sound of claws scraping stone, in what could have been a sign of gratitude, raised almost imperceptibly into his senses.

In the morning, the shape on the chair was more defined. Almost dense enough to touch, and he tries to. But his fingers pass through air, and when he brings this hand to his face, he smells it—the scent of strawberry shampoo. Memories of bath time, late night snuggles, and cartoons in the morning before the rush of school took *her* away.

It was her mother's weekend when she went missing. Abusive boyfriend, his girl's disappearance—an obvious answer to a question everyone besides him stopped asking decades ago. But she wasn't really gone. She was right here on this chair, and in the claws of what was fed nightly in the woods. But, God, what was *her* name again? What was his own?

Carved like ornaments. He wonders what would be carved on these new bones.

* * *

The police began showing up after the third night. Girls disappearing. "They must not have found the bones yet," he wonders aloud when Jonas brings the topic up. There's a look of disgust on Jonas's face and Paul quickly adds, "You know, like with the cats." He can tell everyone suspects him. *Let them*, he thinks. He pictures the ghostly form sitting silently in his room. There was a smile on her face this morning. It won't be much longer until he's done with this work.

THE CONTRACT

Eric Lewis

The minister wandered among gravestones, lost in the dark. The mercenary puffed on his cigar, the flare guiding her to him. "You lied to me."

"What do you mean?" she demanded imperiously. "How dare you summon me here in the middle of—"

"You hired me to stop the strygoi devilling your city. But it was never the city. It was *you*. It wants revenge. For what you did. Yeah, I found out."

"Bastard! So you lured me here for…what? Blackmail?"

"No. Bait." A shadow moved closer in the dark. Moments later, the strygoi was gone, the contract fulfilled.

RESCUED

Gray W. Wolfe

The elves slaughtered the marauding orcs without quarter, without mercy, freeing the village.

"Let us throw you a feast, dear Fae Folk of the Woods," cried the village elder. "It is the least we can do. Let this mark a day of strength between our people and the elves!"

The humans raised their voices in raucous jubilation.

"We accept your generosity," said the elven leader, Niatha. She motioned to her second-in-command.

He approached. "Yes, Commander?"

She whispered, "Feast. Rest. After you've had your fill, slay the men and women, and put their children in chains."

"Your will be done, Commander."

UNHOLY GRACE

Vijayaraj Mahendraraj

The blood-speckled mace slammed against the shield, splitting wood and cracking bone in the arm that absorbed the impact. The woman shrieked, struggling to grip the flailing shield halve. Kneeling and reeling from the blow, she had only a moment to glimpse upward at the glint from his solitary eye before the next blow came thundering down. It smashed the shield fragment, sending splinters into her open face helm. Vicious cuts along her once-unblemished visage and internal bruises left her crumpled, bleeding and gasping in that vast field. The rusted mace was swung back and forth above her, akin to a morbid censer. She dropped her weapon feebly. Her battered makeshift armour gave the assailant pause, a mounting regret. He knew the clumsy girl was no warrior. Probably some maiden who felt the need to protect her family to whatever end, which she too had failed. Blood coated her collar as she coughed up globs of crimson.

"Why?" she whispered in agony.

He towered before her, unflinching, before gazing across the field. It was not a battlefield, but a wheat field. Bodies of commoners lay strewn haphazardly, leading up to the lone house licked by flames. A resounding chapel bell rang nearby. He was burly, three times her size, and bore bulky armour. He was a stranger who entered their lives unannounced and was relentless in their massacre. He crouched by her. She glimpsed an aging soul, a bandana concealing a lost eye. A crude white beard clung to his chiselled jaw, peppered with red.

He spoke in a gruff, yet sympathetic tone, "To the Benevolent One, watch over these souls. He will come to you in your loneliest hour as a vessel to guide you to His homestead, and we, as humble followers, have but to heed the divine call for salvation. Go in peace and suffer this plane no more, child of the One."

Her eyes widened, recounting the familiar words. She fumbled for her weapon, but the mace caved into the side of her helmet, and she remained still forevermore. With the deed done, he entered the barren chapel with his head held low. A statue of the Benevolent One stood proudly, deity to the ailing and foul-fated. The bloodied mace fell from his grasp with a haunting echo. He stared up at the divine face and loosened his armour. The priest's robes beneath were soaked in blood, both fresh and old. His gaze was hollow, mired in misery. A bronze holy chain dangled from his neck.

"When will my penance be paid in full? When will you be appeased with your loyal servant? Have I not demonstrated your unholy grace? Is it the Benevolent One or the Usurper that whispers in my ear? For now, this is all the purpose I have until the day you return my boy to me."

A burly figure left the forlorn chapel and the smouldering homestead that evening to roam the lands in repentance for sins unspoken and deeds unforgiven.

THE ENCHANTED MERMAID

Andreas Hort

He was different.

The mermaid knew it the moment he leaned over deck's edge and saw her in the water. Sailors threw themselves after her into the sea, enamoured of her beauty. Not him.

She met him by the shore near his shack. He asked questions, listened to her answers. Never called her beautiful. She was enchanted. She let him carry her into his shack, put her on his bed. He walked away. Came back grinning, holding a knife.

"One mermaid scale; one gold coin. How rich can you make me, stupid little fish?"

He was different. He was worse.

ONCE MORE INTO THE BREACH

L.J. McLeod

The defences were overrun. The barbarians' numbers were too high to repel. Before night fell, they would all be dead. Horns blared, signalling the withdrawal of the army to the castle's inner keep. Cal fought a running retreat, covering her unit as they covered her in turn. Through the blood, sweat and filth, they had held strong and continued to hold, even with all hope gone.

There was one final option, something so unspeakable that Cal could barely acknowledge it. A spear was thrust at her face, and she only just got her shield up in time. The fighting had raged for hours. Her shield arm was numb, she was exhausted, and she bled from a dozen cuts. Something hard hit her back. She turned to stab it, only to find they had made it to the gate.

The fighting was furious for several more minutes, then they were inside the keep and the gate slammed shut. Archers continued the fight from above, but for a moment she could rest. Cal looked at her broken, bloodied unit. Tam's left arm hung broken and mangled. The twins, Jack and Joe, had several arrows embedded in their bodies. They were working to snap off each other's arrow shafts so they could keep fighting. Naz clutched a bleeding gut wound that would probably be fatal, and Yasmina had a cut right across her beautiful face. If she didn't get it treated soon, she could lose her eye. Cal looked at these people, who meant more to her than family ever had. Even now, she could save them. But it would cost everything. Could she do it?

"Well, it looks like this is finally it gang," Tam said.

"After everything we've been through," Jim sighed.

"At least we all die together," Naz, ever the optimist.

"No!" Cal said. This was it. She had to. "Not here. Not today."

She turned from her friends and ran up the stairs to the top of the wall. All but one of the archers lay dead, or dying. Cal shoved the survivor back down the stairs and turned to face the horde. The barbarian host stretched as far as the eye could see.

Cal had never been special, just an army grunt who swung a sword for a paycheque. But she had one gift, passed down through her bloodline. A death curse, to spend when there was no other choice. She reached down inside herself, to the black flame at her core. It had flickered there her whole life, but now, when she reached for it, it flared.

With a scream, she unleashed that black fire upon the horde. Midnight flames consumed the forward ranks, leaving only ash in their wake. Cal pushed harder, further. There were still so many. The raging fire spread, feeding on her life force for fuel. A final effort of will and the barbarian legion was decimated.

Cal never saw it.

Where she had stood, there were now only embers on the wind.

A Fall in the Hall

Barend Nieuwstraten III

Upon his throne, the lord watched the rebels enter his high-ceilinged hall after they claimed his keep. His houseguard had surrendered their weapons and stood defeated against the walls.

The enemies walked the long white rug triumphantly as the lord watched, smiling. “Before you take my hall,” he said, pointing upwards as the conspirators filled the floor between his great chair and the doors, “I invite you to admire the rafters.”

Up above the invading usurpers, a rookery of men stood silently upon the wooden beams. There was an indoor shower of spears, and the white rug was turned red.

NO LAUGHING MATTER

John H. Dromey

I used to think Grimdark referred to missing a favourite TV sitcom during a power outage. That was *before* my encounter with the Grim Reaper.

The apparition mumbled, “I have the wrong address, but I’ll be back,” before fading away.

I decided then and there, I would not go without a fight. When next the spectre appeared, I planned to strike first.

Statistically speaking, two of the three trick-or-treaters I did away with were imposters. Maybe all three were.

That possibility keeps me awake at night in my padded cell.

What if one of the guards is Death in disguise?

La Petit Mort

Barend Nieuwstraten III

The lord was locked within his own device: a guillotine where trapped hands kept the head company. He'd had his way with several women in this contraption, pulling the cord to end their life so they could finish together.

"A little death brought on by a big one," he'd say. Though they never could confirm, so he didn't know for sure.

A brother of one of his spent ladies, who preferred the company of men, decided to rigorously alleviate that curiosity.

With his ears ringing, he looked back up from the basket, feeling only relief from what was happening before.

THE LAST WARRIOR

Birgit K. Gaiser

A young man stands outside the temple gates.

"Why do you seek the sacred fountain?" I call in my booming contralto.

"I'm hurt," he groans. His sword clashes to the ground. Blood, dried and fresh, stains his tunic.

"Which side are you on?" I ask. "Who's winning?"

He grimaces. "Winning? There's no one left to win."

I beckon towards the life-giving water, but he shimmers, fading into nothingness, like all my ghosts.

I have stood guard for centuries, hoping against hope that there are others somewhere.

I fill my cup and drink deeply. One more day. Tomorrow, someone will come.

A PROUD DEATH

Justin Hunter

The man at the end of his spear began to cry. The sounds of the battlefield surrounding them fading to nothing. There was only the man at the end of his spear. The dying man he would never know. The dying man; his ambitions, fears, and passions, were all dissolving with the passing of his life. He cried, even as his killer struck out his eyes with one swipe of his armoured fingers. He cried still as the man ripped the tongue from his mouth. The silence only came with death, but for the killer, the cries would last forever.

WOLF-BITTEN

Nathan Slemp

My shoulder itches where the wolf's fangs broke my skin. Maybe it's an infection taking root. Or maybe the moonlight is waking something within me.

I stagger down the path back home, unsure if I should turn around. Elaine will be waiting up, a candle in the window for me, expecting me to come home with game.

What am I bringing her? Not the wolf-curse, surely. Just an infection. If I stay away, I'd die alone for no reason.

And even if it is the curse, I wouldn't kill her.

I could never.

Not even as a beast.

Couldn't I?

Diversionary Tactics

Steven Lord

The warrior squinted against the setting sun until he saw the black dot moving steadily towards him. It was close now.

He looked into his son's eyes.

"My lad, I'm going to need you to stay here and hold it off for a while. Do me proud"

He mounted his steed, riding off into the ruins without a backwards glance.

After a few minutes, his pursuer loped up on clawed limbs, a horror from the depths of hell. It skittered to a halt when it saw the swaddled baby, drool dripping from its slavering jaws. Perhaps a quick snack wouldn't hurt.

FOUR DAUGHTERS PROLOGUE

Tim Law

Morticia guided her bone-white mare onward through the icy blizzard. She sensed that her destination, the Temple of Tundra's Might, was close.

"Just a little further, girl," urged Morticia.

Ever trusting, Tria obeyed.

"At last!" Morticia cried, but her triumphant shout was lost to the frozen winds.

Great stone columns betrayed the existence of a path that eons of ice and snow had covered. Carefully, the horse and rider drew nearer until Morticia felt her mount shy. That only happened in the presence of the living; Morticia only had the power to command the undead.

"Who dares to confront a Daughter of Eknos!"

Morticia demanded to know.

"It is I, Daughter of Eknos," quavered a shaven priest as she rushed from the temple entrance and cowered at Morticia's feet. "Shasha, Priestess of Tundra's Might."

"Arise, Shasha!" commanded Morticia. "Arise and act as my guide!"

"As you demand, so shall I obey," replied the priestess.

Wrapped in furs, Morticia dismounted and followed the priestess, noting how nibble of foot the lithe figure was. It was as if the creature felt not the biting cold, nor the slipperiness of the tundra. Like a dark shade, the priestess fled ahead.

"Halt! I order you to halt!" commanded Morticia.

The Daughter of Eknos searched for death, any death that lingered within the harsh ice and snow. Death that she could pull up from the unforgiving earth and manipulate like a puppeteer. The tundra was empty. Not a single soul awaited the necromancer's summoning.

"Come! Come and follow!" Laughed the priestess.

Morticia hurried and almost tumbled, but her inner strength helped her to retain her footing. Within the darkness of the temple, the wild winds ceased and there was silence. Far away, the laughter of Shasha could be heard. There was another presence, also, that Morticia could detect; perhaps the essence of Tundra's Might, the very essence she had come here to claim for herself.

"Sister Morticia!" cried a voice, a voice Morticia knew all too well. "You are too late."

Thaea, sorceress and Commander of the Elements, stood beside the altar upon which lay the ice crystal—the heart of the temple. Beside her, kneeling in worship, was Shasha.

“I should have slain you when I saw you, traitor!” announced Morticia.

Claw-like fingers stretched forth, and a dark, foreboding essence drifted from the necromancer towards the prostrate priestess.

“Save me, mistress!” begged Shasha of Thaea.

Too late though, the dark tendrils made their way into the priestess’ eyes and ears and tore at her soul.

“You are mine, now,” Morticia stated.

As if from a silent command, the fresh corpse arose and began clawing at Thaea.

Morticia turned and fled, knowing full well that one soulless ghoul would be insufficient to keep the Elementalist, Thaea, at bay.

“Stay and play, sister!” called Thaea as she pulled stalactites from the temple ceiling, the icy spears slicing through Shasha and pinning the priestess to the temple floor.

Thaea turned to strike again, but Morticia was already gone.

Four Daughters Prophecy

Tim Law

Four daughters all born from one mother
Each has vowed to destroy all the others
A battle to claim the ultimate prize
A hunt for a father who remains in disguise
One sister holds the power of might
Destiny predicts she'll win every fight
Another sister has the gift of elemancy
Able to command earth, sky, fire, and sea
Sister three wields charisma with remiss
Adding to her forces with each man she chooses to kiss
The last sister lives in shade
Awakening those who to rest have been laid
A mother's love, jealousy destroys
Sisters become a father's toys

Four Daughters The Game

Tim Law

Jo woke up groggy, finding herself on the cold, hard floor of a cell. She ached all over, but it was the back of her head that hurt the most.

"Back here again," she grumbled. "How the hell did I get here this time?"

Thinking back, Jo vaguely recalled reuniting with her unit somewhere in Hurikkan Forest, two or three days from home. If she was back in the Game, that meant they were all dead; Danny, Mick, Sofia the Shadow, and the rest of her unit, all gone. Jo held back a single tear and breathed in deep. What she needed was a stiff drink and a large helping of revenge. The revenge would need to come first, and for that, Jo knew she needed out of the cell. In the gloom, she felt around and found, under the bench seat, a wooden blade. Last time they'd left her a steel bar, and the times before there had been a bunch of other items far more useful than the equivalent of a sharp stick. At least as weapons went, it seemed solid, a single piece; blade, hilt, and handle, all carved as one. The blade was sharp along one edge, surprisingly so for a piece of wood. The weight of the weapon was impressive too—Jo assumed Stone Tree wood from Othiu Forest located at the base of the Gaithu Ranges.

On the bench seat, Jo found a breastplate, a pair of gauntlets, and some leather sandals. Someone was having a joke at her expense. Anyone who knew her, and knew of her reputation, understood Captain Jo Herald never wore sandals. She always preferred boots, metal-capped because that kind of boot was great for kicking in doors. Dressed in what she'd been given, even the sandals, Jo slid the sword into its sheath and tried the cell door. It moved silently, well-oiled, looked after, but it did not swing open. Jo gave the bars a kick near the hinges and immediately regretted that decision.

"Bloody sandals," Jo cursed.

There came a gurgle of laughter from the cell across from Jo.

"I would have thought better judgment from you, Captain," stated a familiar voice.

"Theo! Did they get you, too?"

"Sadly, yes." Laughter drained away, replaced with self-pity. "I was just leaving the gambling hall of King Maa's Crystal Palace."

"You were counting your winnings before you even left the casino, weren't you?" Jo accused.

"Yes," Theo admitted. "I was arrogant. I have paid the price."

"Let's hope it isn't the ultimate price," muttered Jo.

"What weapon have you been given?" Theo asked. "I have a length of chain."

"It seems they don't trust me with real weapons," replied Jo. "I've got a sharp stick."

Theo laughed again, a booming roar that made obvious his size.

"Captain Herald, I do believe they want you to die."

"They love me here," Jo protested sarcastically. "Why else would they continue to ask me back again?"

"Perhaps they love you, or maybe they just want another go at snuffing you out…" suggested Theo.

Jo could hear the giant's shoulders shrug, even though she couldn't see him.

"How long is your chain?" Jo asked. "See if you can slide it across the passage to my cell."

There was a rattle as Theo attempted, first a slide and then a throw. On the third go, several chain-links made it into Jo's cell. Wrapping what she had around the bars, Jo forced her blade through a couple of links.

"Now pull," she commanded, meanwhile praying the chain and sword would hold.

The chain threatened to break; the links twisting with a faint whine of protest.

Theo grunted from across the way, and suddenly the

door was pulled free. Jo stepped through the opening with a triumphant grin.

Untangling the chain from the sword, Jo cursed as she noted a great crack along the shaft of her weapon. She let the useless wood clatter to the floor and focused on Theo.

"Thanks, Theo, I owe you," Jo admitted.

"At my count, it is five you owe me, now," rumbled the giant.

There was a hint of humour as the giant replied, but it was not the same joyous chortle as before.

Looking around, Jo discovered a wooden beam above her head. Throwing the length of chain over, and then wrapping its remaining length around the useless wooden sword, she handed the bundle back through the cell to Theo. The giant grunted as he heaved with all of his mighty strength. Both chain and cell bars screamed in protest until the chain finally gave way.

"Damn!" Jo and Theo stated together.

"You almost paid me back once, anyway," rumbled the giant.

In the semidarkness, Jo could see the bars were lifted enough for her to roll underneath and back into Theo's cell. Far away, the pair could hear sounds of approach—the thump of three or four pairs of boots drawing nearer and nearer.

"Move aside," demanded Jo as she dropped to the passage floor. "I swear I'm going to get you out of this cell."

"By joining me in it?" queried the giant. "Captain

Herald, if you were anyone else I would call you a fool."

"Hush!" murmured Jo as she rolled under the prison cell door.

Moments later, four soldiers, all dressed in black leathers, appeared, pausing at the open doorway of the cell Captain Jo Herald had just vacated. Jo and Theo knew these were soldiers of Sorcerer Kalliha, the mastermind behind the Game. At the hip of each soldier, there hung a crossbow. The bolts would be tipped with poison, some designed to cause slumber, and some designed to quickly kill.

"Beware," ordered one of the guards.

Three crossbows were swiftly loaded, cranked, and then raised to eye level.

The guard captain pulled a tube from his backpack, which he then cracked before throwing it in, illuminating the cell. Eager eyes searched the interior, including the ceiling. There was nowhere to hide.

"She isn't in there," rumbled Theo.

As one, the guards and crossbows all trained on his voice.

The longest part of what remained of the chain flicked out from the darkness and knocked one guard. His crossbow fired sideways, scoring a fellow guard in the helmet.

"Fire!" ordered the head guard, and the final loaded crossbow trigger was pulled.

Theo groaned and fell to the cell floor.

There came the sound of a bunch of keys as the head

guard opened up Theo's cell door.

"Go check on him," the guard ordered of the one who had shot his comrade.

Shaking hands placed the crossbow away before swinging open the cell door.

The giant's hand shot out and crushed the guard's face.

"Thanks," whispered Jo as she leaped over Theo's bulk and skipped out of his cell.

One guard remained; the one who had been giving out the orders.

"Do we want to try the hard way or…?" Captain Herald queried.

She nodded as the guard began to draw his short sword from its hilt.

"Good choice," Jo said.

In a flash, she had bridged the gap between her and the soldier and rammed the flat of her hand into the bridge of his nose. The soldier had been almost handsome before the blow, but Jo's strike had deformed him. As he brought a feeble hand up to his face, Jo disarmed him. The sword clattered on the stone floor before she picked it up and stabbed the man.

"Where does my sister find you all?" Jo wondered.

These guys had not been well trained, if they were, in fact, trained at all.

Searching the guys with the crossbows, Jo found a tube of antidote.

"Wake up, Theo!" she cried as she tried to force the

liquid in the tube down the giant's throat.

"Aaaaaaaarrrrrgggghhhhhh…" groaned Theo as his eyes fluttered.

"There, look," Jo urged as she pointed out the open cell door. "Brought you back to life and got you out of this cage."

"Agreed," Theo groaned as he brought stumpy fingers to his temples and rubbed vigorously.

"I would say that is worth at least five," Jo said with a grin. "So now you're on your own."

A ghostly image of Sorcerer Kalliha appeared in the corridor. Jo had seen this image enough times already to know it wasn't real.

"*Brava! Brava*, little sister," the image cried. "You have caught the interest of our viewers already."

"Little sister?" spat back Captain Herald. "We are quadruplets. You are only ten minutes older."

"Older is still older," said the arcane image. "Not that we have time for small talk."

"Time to go," Jo murmured. "Nice seeing you."

A scraping sound that couldn't be heard before was now quickly drawing nearer. Jo kicked off her sandals, then stole the boots from the soldier she had killed. He no longer needed them. They weren't a great fit, but they were boots. Jo had a feeling there would be doors down the track that would need kicking in.

"Good luck, Theo," Jo called as she ran down the corridor away from the sound. "Hopefully we both make it to the end."

“Indeed,” Theo rumbled as he pulled himself to his feet.

Waddling slowly out of the cell, he reached up and yanked on the beam in the ceiling. Jo stopped running long enough to glance back. The ceiling collapsed, causing Theo to disappear from sight. It also opened up a precarious stairway to the upper levels.

“Looks like I owe you again.” Jo laughed as she turned about-face and headed upwards.

The climb up was an easy one for such an experienced warrior as Captain Jo Herald. She avoided more guards who had rushed to the scene and navigated the maze of corridors to arrive at the throne room doors within half an hour. With one swift kick, the double doors flew open. There within, Jo found her sister, Sorcerer Kalliha, flanked by ten armoured knights.

“You are first to arrive, Captain Herald. Father would be proud,” purred the sorcerer.

Jo looked on in disgust as her sister lounged across the bejewelled throne like it was nothing but a day bed. Kalliha was dressed, as usual, in almost nakedness; a costume she used regularly, and well, to draw all men close enough that they could taste her lips. That was the way the spider grew her army. Each day, more and more fools came searching, thinking they would claim Kalliha’s heart. Each suitor failed in this impossible quest, instead they merely added to the sorcerer’s field of fodder.

“First to arrive, so I have won your silly game, sister,” cried Jo triumphantly.

"Not this time. First to arrive merely means the first to die."

With a snap of her fingers, the sorcerer caused the knights to animate. Spear tips were lowered, longswords were drawn. Jo noticed one knight wielded a ball and chain, the spiked ball reminding Jo of Kalliha's dark heart. The first knight swung down with his blade, Jo easily deflecting it with her own. As she made to stab, Captain Herald found she needed to twist out of the path of a spearhead. Another spear caught her across the stomach, while a longsword blade sliced through her leathers and nicked her under the ribs.

"This time, sister…this time I will end you," vowed Kalliha.

"Nay, Sorcerer, you are wrong," replied Jo as she stole the ball and chain.

With two weapons in such skilled hands, the knights fell c. Finally, there were only two who remained in the throne room. Jo stood panting, cuts and bruises covering her every limb.

"You cannot enchant me, sister," said Captain Herald with a smile. "Hand over the Triple Crown."

Gore and crimson dripped from the short blade while the head of the ball and chain remained stuck in the face of one knight's helm.

"I do not need to cast my spells upon you, Josephine," Sorcerer Kalliha said, laughing.

At that moment, Theo lumbered into the throne room.

"Captain Herald," he cried in delight.

"There are always men," stated Sorcerer Kalliha confidently.

"I have won!" demanded Jo. "Hand over the prize."

"Theo the Giant, please kill my sister," commanded the sorcerer.

"With pleasure," rumbled Theo.

"Theo, I am destined to win," pleaded Jo. "I do not wish to kill you."

"But kill me you must," announced the giant. "Else I'll crush you first."

Upon every wall of the throne room, mirrors appeared, revealing the crowd who watched on. Theo soaked up their cheers, while Jo did her best to ignore the distraction. As the giant lunged at her, Jo stepped aside and stabbed. Theo's roar of pain turned into a laugh—a hollow, and deep laugh so unlike the natural chortle of the giant. Each time the giant attempted to grasp Jo and crush her, she was able to dance out of the way. Sometimes she could stab and slice, but more often it was difficult enough to keep out of reach. More warriors steamed in, more men, each one giving Jo a glazed-over look before bowing towards the enchanter.

"Kill her!" Sorcerer Kalliha urged of each new arrival.

Each warrior promised they would be the one. Captain Herald somehow managed to avoid the worst of the attacks, taking shallow cuts and scratches on her arms and legs. As if fate wanted her to live, Jo slipped in blood pools as axes flew by her, dodged out of the way of a swinging chain. Warrior killed warrior to make sure they could be the one. When a clawed monstrosity tore out Theo's face, Jo saw red.

"Kill her! Kill her now!" screeched Kalliha.

With each warrior Jo managed to vanquish, the sorcerer's cries became more and more desperate. The crowd's chanting became fever pitched as Jo faced off with the final foe. The floor ran red with a thin wash of blood, as carefully Jo stalked a dwarf. The fellow's beard and boots were spattered red. His axe was twice the size of him—a poor weapon for an indoor fight, and yet a weapon he had proven he could wield well.

"Give up now, lass," the dwarf rumbled. "I be the greatest warrior of my clan."

"And who be your clan?" asked Jo, innocently.

"I be Johanni, Son of Gerrard the Mad, Son of Redwolf of the East Mist Mountains, Son of…"

Captain Herald watched for the moment when the dwarf's mind left the skirmish, as he tried valiantly to recall his heritage.

"No, you fool!" cursed the sorcerer.

Jo made a leap of faith, somehow covering the distance between her and the dwarf without slipping. With a longblade in one hand, and a woodsman's axe in the other, Jo swung and stabbed. The dwarf, Johanni, brought about his great weapon, but Jo was much faster. The tip of the longsword parted the bushy beard and pierced the warrior's neck, while the woodsman's axe did half the job of lopping the dwarf's head from his shoulders. As the dead stayed standing in shock, Jo came around with a backhanded blow, axe and sword joining forces to finish the job. The head slid with a sickening sound before it landed at the feet of Sorcerer Kalliha with a faint splat.

"Give up sister, you have no more of your mindless men to throw at me," demanded Jo.

"You are right," moaned Kalliha. "You always seem to win our fights; the Gods seem to smile upon you while they laugh at me behind my back."

The sorcerer kicked away the dwarf's head before she slid from the throne to kneel at Jo's feet.

"Your knees, your feet, your beauty are bathed in blood," said Jo.

"We are born in blood, and in the glory of blood so we wish to die," announced Kalliha. "Take my head, sister, if that be the prize that you seek."

"I wish not for your throne, sister," answered Captain Herald. "I just want what I have rightfully earned, our father's crown that rests upon your head."

As Jo claimed the crown, she heard a whisper. There was something not right, something strange. Sorcerer Kalliha looked at Jo as if she hoped her secrets were safe. There was a moment when Kalliha took hold of Jo's hands, as if wanting to stop her from taking the crown, but the gesture was weak. Everything about Kalliha was strength through beauty and manipulation. Without the men to dance upon her deceitful webbing, the sorcerer had no power left.

"Let go," Jo urged gently. "The battle is over, and you have lost."

With a wave of her hand, Kalliha dismissed the mirrors, and the sound of the crowd ceased.

"Yes, I have lost the battle," admitted the enchanter. "But I have not lost the war."

With one final trick, Sorcerer Kalliha vanished from sight, leaving Jo alone with the dead, the throne, and the Triple Crown. As she made to place her prize upon her head, again Jo heard the whispers.

"Release me," begged the voice. "Please release me from this prison…"

With a blow of fury, Jo smashed the crown upon the throne. From within the broken pieces rose up a ghostly wisp, a pale apparition that became the image of Eknos, father of the four daughters.

"The true crown is waiting to be claimed," the image announced. "Seek it out upon the Planet of Pain."

Phantom

Vijayaraj Mahendraraj

The terrified panting intensified. The barred door splintered, a cacophony of curses outside.

"It's over! It's here!"

A group of guards burst into the ramshackle hut, raising their weapons before hesitating.

"It's just a…boy," said one.

"Aye! Where's it gone?" asked another.

Tears streamed down the child's face. The group departed, bitterly resuming the search, except one, who knelt.

"Are you alright?"

The boy kept mumbling, "I can't. I can't."

"Let's get you somewhere safe," he replied, turning.

"I can't stop it!"

A giant phantasmal maw clenched down over half the guard's body, and no one heard the screams.

END GAME

Lee Hammerschmidt

"So, he finally cracked, did he, Lutefisk?" Colonel Plegmovitch asked his chief interrogator.

"Yes sir," Lieutenant Lutefisk said. "But he was a tough and determined bastard. He withstood all of our most gruelling torture techniques. Clamps, electrodes, rubber hoses, pukka shells, waterboarding, Barry Manilow music. You name it, he was able to endure it. So, we took off the kid gloves and brought out the heavy artillery, and he sang like a canary. We know everything the rebels have planned."

"Heavy artillery…you didn't!" Plegmovitch exclaimed in horror. "Lutefisk you sick, twisted fuck!"

"Yes! We forced him to play Yahtzee!"

A CHANGE OF UNIFORM

Birgit K. Gaiser

Hanno wiped his bloody face with his sleeve, adding to the collection of bodily fluids soaked into the fabric.

He recalled the drills, all the talk of glory, brotherhood. How naive he'd been. His "brothers" lay dead on the ground a short walk away.

The enemy soldier who had been chasing him was badly wounded. Hanno could leave now. And yet… Looking at the man, his clothing—with a uniform like that, he might make it all the way to the border, maybe talk a farmer out of meal, or even a horse.

Hanno pulled his dagger and bent down.

RETURNING THE FAVOUR

Blen

Surrender or die: those were the only options he had given me back then. I had picked the former, for the time being at least. Dying then wouldn't have done me any good.

I never liked the sound of either option—they were quite a no-win situation for me—so I made my own: revenge. I wouldn't have let him get away with it, not in a million years. He will find out soon enough that his family is no more, but it's only fair, is it not?

He had destroyed my world, whereas I was simply returning the favour.

JUNKERS

William Bartlett

Drifter on the unforgiving sea
carried from one wave to the next
pushed by the current of my own past
consequences eventually leaving me stranded
ashore a lonely island.
I explore the only island on this world
a junkyard stretching from shore to shore
the world's discarded and broken things
rusted from the mist of the sea's ridicule
gypsies and tinkerers
psychics and oddballs
exiles of normalcy, just like me.
on this island of junk
I could love freely
we'd find and understand each other
junker king and junker queen of nothing

nothing to the sea
but everything to me.

NO QUARTER

Jameson Grey

Flies flitted indecisively between fresh horse shit and the prisoner's remains.

Parry had been hanged, drawn, and beheaded already. The executioner had cleaved his body in twain and set about repeating the task for each half. His protective mask slipped, and he gagged, stepping aside momentarily to dry heave.

Günter waited with the three other riders. To his end, Parry had shielded knowledge of Günter's part in the plot to kill the king. Now, it was Günter's duty to transport a quarter of Parry's corpse to the kingdom's far northeast.

There'd be time yet to brood on thoughts of treason.

CANNIBALISM DAY

Andrew Kurtz

Jack witnessed a man disembowelling a woman and eating her internal organs. The blood gushing from the woman's mouth as she screamed was collected and used as a jus for her organs.

"Don't eat the heart—it tastes bitter and can give you indigestion," Jack shouted, playfully holding his belly and pretending to vomit.

After, he walked past three men roasting a newborn over a blazing fire, its loud wails fading to silence as they cut off thick rump chunks with knives.

"Best add salt, otherwise the flesh will taste dry!" Jack yelled at them.

"Excuse me, young man, I have only been in town a few days and I'm appalled at what I am seeing," an elderly man with a cane admonished Jack.

"It is National Cannibalism Day. One day every year,

people are allowed to eat other people. I saw a man eating a woman's severed breast on Italian bread with mayonnaise and American cheese. I suggested he wash it down with some urine, but he didn't quite appreciate the humour." Jack giggled.

"I find the whole thing repulsive. I'm staying just a few blocks away—would like you to join me for a delicious, juicy steak dinner with mashed potatoes, drowned in hot gravy?" the man offered.

"Allow me to make sure I look presentable," Jack responded, examining himself using a small pocket mirror.

"You seem to enjoy this special day. Do you eat people as well?" the man asked.

"Hell, no! I just enjoy mocking them. However, there is one thing that I loathe about today," Jack said while in the process of kicking a wooden picket fence and carrying one of the planks.

"Why did you do that, and what do you hate?" asked the man, surprised by Jack's actions.

"You never know what you will run into on a night like this, and I will tell you at dinner what I detest tonight," Jack responded.

The old man's house could have passed for a museum. There were ancient statues from the time of Plato, and original paintings from painters who were now nothing but ash.

"Where did you get all this stuff?" Jack asked, wide-eyed.

"I never answer questions on an empty stomach. Let's

eat and then we'll talk," the man said in a deeper voice than Jack noticed before.

The kitchen was bare except for a refrigerator and a wooden table.

"All year I have concealed my existence by drinking bottled animal blood, but during this holiday I treat myself to fresh human blood." The vampire dropped his cane, and with wings springing out of his back, flew at Jack.

"You invited me over for a steak dinner, but instead, you are getting a stake," Jack said and rammed the wooden plank into the vampire's chest.

"Ahhhhh!" screamed the vampire, his flesh beginning to disintegrate, revealing a yellow, crumbling skeleton.

"I love Cannibalism Day, but I hate the fact that vampires interfere with the festivities." Jack laughed at the pile of vampire ashes.

THE RIGHT THING

Blen

The hospital rejected sick people every day. Most beds had patients with an unknown virus. On a scale of one to ten, each one described their pain as a ten.

Ivan worked day and night, trying—and failing—to give patients the slightest relief. He knew a cure wouldn't be discovered for months. He knew he would be sentenced if he got caught. But he also knew that he had to do the right thing.

The next day, every patient with the virus was dead, relieved of their misery. Nobody uncovered what happened.

It was the right thing to do.

TURNING THE TIDE

Birgit K. Gaiser

Nadin raised the scroll, its letters blazing a red warning.

Raising the dead was risky under any circumstances. Raising a mad witch with powers unmatched in centuries was foolish at best, suicidal at worst. Still, they had little choice. The enemy was winning.

Without the witch, they were almost certainly dead. With her—it was a chance.

Nadin started the invocation. Immediately, anger and hatred tore into their body, threatening to destroy them. They struggled against the tide, screaming the words. The witch's silhouette appeared in the sky, cackling, raising her hands.

Nadin sank to their knees.

The witch struck.

FRIEND

Justin Hunter

It is folly to forgive. It is a weakness to forget. His eyes darken around the edges as he drives his steel home. There is the crunch of bone followed by the sickly wet sound of entrails spilling upon the ground. He watches the eyes of his victim—his friend—as they dim. The dying opens his mouth. No words come. No rebuke. That soundless open maw will forever haunt the victor as he will wonder from this day until he breathes his last—

What was the man going to say? Will he ever know why he had to die?

ASSASSIN

Blen

It wasn't as if Luke wanted this. He needed it to survive. He knew right from the start getting into the business was trouble. And he could leave with the small price of his life.

His life, at the cost of innocent victims. The only thing that got Luke out of bed was deluding himself into believing that was fair.

But as he sank his blade into another victim, it got harder to believe.

That night, Luke went to bed, pretending nothing out of the ordinary had happened. He would never be able to sleep if he faced his actions.

GONE WORLD

R.S. Nevil

"It was not always like this."

The old man's words echoed in the silence.

"Once upon a time, life was great. Our food was abundant. And the sun rose every day."

"And what happened to that world?" Gregor accused. "You squandered it. Your foolishness cost the rest of us our chance of living such a life. And now we are stuck here. Barely scraping by."

The old man shook his head. It was not his foolishness that had cost them. It had been the arrogance of his people. He didn't see it now.

But one day the boy would understand.

THE STORY OF MARCOS

R.S. Nevil

The blue light spread for as far as the eye could see.

It was hypnotic, the light once a major attraction. That attraction no longer held, though. The great flood had seen to that.

Now, it was a place where people went to die. People like him. People who were exiled.

It was the ultimate prison world, a world with no way of surviving. No food. No water. No shelter. Only the promise of death remained.

This was where he had been sent. And it would be where the final chapter of his story was told.

The story of Marcos.

An Ounce of Humanity

John H. Dromey

A star ship commander quizzed his chief engineer. "Will the androids we're transporting behave themselves on Earth?"

"Yes, sir. Each of them has exactly one-sixteenth of a pound of homo-sapiens-compatible genetic material infused into its artificial intelligence component. They'll treat humans with respect and dignity."

Later...

"Captain! Remember the crewman who complained about being assigned menial tasks while our cargo hold is filled with capable androids?"

"What about him?"

"He activated one of the units and released it from its restraints. It's a killing machine."

“How’s that possible?” the captain asked.

“Our ship’s artificial gravity is only three-quarters Earth normal.”

Get to the Point!

Andrew Kurtz

The vampire approached Dale, fangs dripping with blood and carrying the severed head of his female victim.

"I have drained all the blood from your wife. You're next to die!" the vampire threatened menacingly.

A smile grew across Dale's face as he pointed up at the night sky.

"You smile now, but you'll be screaming momentarily." The vampire laughed and lunged at Dale.

A hairy arm grasped the vampire's neck, and as the vampire was being torn to shreds by razor-sharp claws, he realised that Dale was pointing at the full moon.

The werewolf enjoyed his feast of vampire flesh.

THE GUY WITH A LIFE'S MISSION

Christopher T. Dabrowski

He loved to fight for the rights of the oppressed. He whose life mission was to be good.

He saved animals, helped the poor, and chained himself to the trees. He was protecting, saving, and helping.

People admired him. Everyone wanted to be his friend. Women dreamt about him.

Then everything changed.

The world became good.

But he, instead of being happy, felt very sad. No one got hurt, so there was no one to save.

He felt unnecessary, even though people admired and loved him.

So he decided he would change too—from now on he

would be bad!

LAST ORDERS

James Hancock

After three exhausting months of blood, mud, and constant rain, General Varund ended the siege. His army ceased the relentless bombardment that very night and moved south to the coast. His captains were instructed to organise the retreat, for he had personal matters to attend. Never question the general's orders.

The night before, three hooded figures had found their way to General Varund's personal latrine and taken him by surprise. They knew he'd never call off the attack, so there was only one thing for it. An actor stepped in for a one-night performance, and the general was carefully skinned.

DRAB

Olen Crowe

The mud and shit had long mixed together into a singular brown slop.

Wallowing in their own filth. It would have made for a perfect metaphor, had it not been their morning, noon, and night for the past season.

The rain wouldn't stop.

The whispers saying that help would arrive soon had long ceased. All contact had ceased, save for the bread boy. He replenished their bucket with stale bread. The other bucket collected rainwater when Edward's fits didn't kick the damned thing over.

Grey skies. Grey stone. Grey chains.

Here comes the man in the black hood.

It's over.

A PLACE TO CALL HOME

Vijayaraj Mahendraraj

"Halt!"

"Please, we are refugees. Our homes were burnt in wars of nobler folk with lesser minds. We seek a home," they pleaded.

"We can't house all of you. Too many mouths," the guard replied.

"Permit us to stay tonight, out of the rain. We beg you."

The villagers agreed.

They huddled beneath nooks and sheltered roofs. As thunder claimed the night, they crept into each house with concealed blades.

The guard woke the next morning, alone amidst a sea of dead brethren and a shovel at his feet.

"Welcome to our new home. I hope you're good at digging."

AUTHOR SHOWCASE

William Bartlett

William Bartlett identifies as a dark poet, sword-and-sorcery fantasy author, gothic short story writer, editor with Quill & Crow Publishing House, and a dragon currently in its human form. Oh yea, and also as a lump of love.

Twitter: @wbartlett1984

Blen

Blen is an Ethiopian writer who spends her free time surfing on the internet for hours on end. Writing is a way for her to express herself through characters she will, unfortunately, never meet. You can find her on Twitter: @blen4321.

Maggie D. Brace

Maggie D Brace, a lifelong denizen of Maryland, teacher, gardener, basketball player and author attended St. Mary's College, where she met her soulmate, and Loyola University, Maryland. She has written *'Tis Himself: The Tale of Finn MacCool* and *Grammy's Glasses* and has multiple short works and poems in various anthologies. She remains a humble scrivener and avid reader

Olen Crowe

Olen was born in the Appalachian foothills of North Carolina, but he now lives in Chattanooga, Tennessee with his wife and two children. Besides reading and writing, he likes to hike, watch cheesy B-horror movies, and study linguistics.

Christopher T. Dabrowski

Christopher T. Dabrowski was born in Poland in 1978 year. He has stories published in *Anomaly* (2019, Royal Hawaiian Press), *Escape* (2019, Royal Hawaiian Press), *Anomalia* (2019, Royal Hawaiian Press), *La fuga* (2019, Royal Hawaiian Press), *Deathbirth* (2008, Armoryka), and many more.

Facebook:Krzysztof-T-Dąbrowski-166581686751600

John H. Dromey

John H. Dromey was born in northeast Missouri, USA. He enjoys reading—mysteries in particular—and writing in a variety of genres. John contributed five drabbles to each of the first ten anthologies in the Black Hare Press Dark Drabbles series. Two of his drabbles are online in *Dark Moments*.

Birgit K. Gaiser

Birgit lives in Edinburgh, Scotland and writes short speculative fiction. They enjoy the slightly bizarre, and characters who view the world with a healthy dose of sarcasm. They like to consult their PhD in toxicology for the occasional (literary) poisoning.

You can find them on Facebook: BirgitKGaiser

Xavier Garcia

Xavier Garcia is a writer/editor from Toronto, Canada. His short fiction work has been previously published by Black Hare Press, and a short horror film he wrote/produced won the Best Film award at the Rue Morgue and Sinister Nights Film Festival.

R. Wayne Gray

R. Wayne Gray is a Vermont-based writer who has published in a wide range of genres and formats. His short fiction has recently appeared in Cosmic Horror Monthly, Trembling With Fear, and the anthologies 666 Dark Drabbles and Bloody Good Horror.

Twitter: @RWayneGray

Website: www.rwaynegray.com

Jameson Grey

Jameson Grey is originally from England but now lives with his family in western Canada. His work has been published in *Dark Dispatch, The Birdseed*, and anthologies from Ghost Orchid Press, Black Ink Fiction, and Hellbound Books.

Website: jameson-grey.com

Lee Hammerschmidt

Lee Hammerschmidt is a Visual Artist/Writer/Troubadour who lives in Oregon. He is the author of the short story collections, *A Hole Of My Own* and *It's Noir O'clock Somewhere*. Check out his hit parade on YouTube!

www.youtube.com/user/MrLeehammer

James Hancock

James Hancock is a writer/screenwriter of comedy, thriller, horror, sci-fi and twisted fairy tales. A few of his short screenplays have been made into films, and he has been published in print magazines, online, and in anthology books.

He lives in England, with his wife and two daughters. And a bunch of pets he insisted his girls could NOT have.

Toko Hata

Toko Hata is a writer based in Tokyo, Japan. Some of her horror drabbles have been published by Ghost Orchid Press and Trembling with Fear. Find her at @hata_toko on twitter.

Liam Hogan

Liam Hogan is an award-winning short story writer, with stories in *Best of British Science Fiction* and in *Best of British Fantasy* (NewCon Press). He's been published by Analog, Daily Science Fiction, and Flame Tree Press, among others. He helps host Liars' League London, volunteers at the creative writing charity Ministry of Stories, and lives and avoids work in London. More details at happyendingnotguaranteed.blogspot.co.uk

Andreas Hort

Andreas Hort is a Czech author writing in English. At nine, he began scribbling comics with pencils. Later, he decided that he preferred drawing the scenes with his words. He never stopped writing, and somewhere along the way, he started getting paid for it. Contact him on Twitter: @TheAndreasHort.

Justin Hunter

Justin Hunter is an author from Missouri, USA.

Andrew Kurtz

Andrew Kurtz is an up-and-coming horror author who writes very graphic and violent short stories which have appeared in numerous horror anthologies.

Since childhood, he has loved horror films and literature.

His favourite authors are Stephen King, Clive Barker, H.G. Wells, Richard Matheson, Edgar Allan Poe, H.P. Lovecraft, and Ray Bradbury.

John Lane

John Lane's fiction has appeared in Black Hare Press, Ghost Orchid Press, Black Ink Fiction, Crow's Feet Journal, Dark Dossier Magazine, dyst Literary Journal and other venues. John's fiction has also appeared in several literary publications.

John's story about a tragic playground incident was featured on the Hyakumonogatari Kaidankai: 100 Days, 100 Supernatural Stories podcast, and he is a member of the Horror Writers Association.

Tim Law

Tim Law hides behind a keyboard hoping that his family and friends do not discover the darkness that swirls about in his mind whispering promises and secrets. The secrets are growing louder though and the promises, well some promises are difficult to resist.

Eric Lewis

By day Eric Lewis is the author of *The Heron Kings*, available from Flame Tree Press. His short fiction has been published in *Nature, Cossmass Infinities, Bards & Sages Quarterly*, the anthology *Crash Code*, the short story *collection As It Seems*, and many other venues detailed at ericlewis.ink.

A. Lily

A. Lily is a speculative fiction author and has been published by Black Hare Press, amongst others.

Steven Lord

Steven Lord is a fantasy and sci-fi author from the UK. His influences include Neal Stephenson, Stephen King, and Iain M. Banks. Steven currently lives in London with his wife, dog, and two cats, and is resigned to his place at the bottom of the pecking order in the house...

Vijayaraj Mahendraraj

Vijayaraj Mahendraraj, who goes by Vijay, is originally from Malaysia but currently works as a physician in Canada. Writing has always been a burning passion of theirs, and, having few prior publications, it is something they constantly strive towards.

L.J. McLeod

L.J. McLeod lives in Queensland, Australia. She works in Pathology and writes in her spare time. She has been published in several anthologies and has been nominated twice for the Aurealis Award. In her spare time, she enjoys diving, reading and travelling.

Mike Murphy

Mike has had over 150 audio plays produced in the US and overseas, and has won the Columbine Award, the inaugural Marion Thauer Brown Audio Drama Scriptwriting Competition, and a dozen Moondance International Film Festival awards in various categories. His prose has appeared in several magazines and anthologies. In 2020, his screenplay *Die Laughing* was a semi-finalist in the Unique Voices Screenplay Competition from *Creative Screenwriting Magazine*. His TV pilot script, "The Bullying Squad," was a quarterfinalist in the *Emerging Writers* Genre Screenplay Competition. He is also the writer of two short films, *Dark Chocolate* and *Hotline*.

For several of the in-between years, he served as a judge.

Blog: audioauthor.blogspot.com.

R.S. Nevil

R.S. Nevil is an avid reader and author. He mainly writes science fiction, while also dabbling in other genres. R.S. spends most of his free time reading, writing, and trying to perfect his craft, coming up with new and fantastic tales of Werewolves, Vampires, and anything else Supernatural.

Barend Nieuwstraten III

Barend Nieuwstraten III grew up and lives in Sydney, Australia, where he was born to Dutch and Indian immigrants. He has worked in film, short film, television, music, and online comics. He is now primarily working on a collection of stories set within a high fantasy world, a science fiction alternate future, as well as a steampunk storyverse, often dipping his toes in horror in the process. With over twenty short stories published in anthologies, he continues to work on short stories, stand-alone novels, and an epic series.

Facebook: https://www.facebook.com/Barend3Author

Blog: https://barend3.blogspot.com

Michelle Chermaine Ramos

Michelle Chermaine Ramos is a multidisciplinary artist, poet, writer, and journalist in Toronto, Canada. Raised in the U.A.E and being of Filipino, Spanish and Japanese descent, her art weaves different cultural threads to reveal magic in everyday life.

Instagram: @michellechermaine.

Daniel R. Robichaud

Daniel R. Robichaud lives and writes in Humble, Texas. His fiction has been collected in *Hauntings & Happenstances: Autumn Stories* and Gathered *Flowers, Stones, and Bones: Fabulist Stories*. Keep up with him on Facebook, @daniel.r.robichaud. He also writes weekly reviews at consideringstories.wordpress.com.

D.L. Shirey

D.L. Shirey lives in Portland, Oregon under skies the colour of bruises. Occasionally he lightens up, but his dark fiction can be found in *Confingo, Zetetic, Liquid Imagination* and in anthologies from Truth Serum Press and Literary Hatchet. Find more of his writing at www.dlshirey.com and @dlshirey on Twitter.

Nathan Slemp

When not conversing with dragons and chronicling their tales, Nathan Slemp spends his time as a software developer in Michigan. His short stories can be found in the *Fairytale Dragons* anthology by Dragon Soul Press, and upcoming in *Flash Point SF*. Other works and musings can be found at wordwyrm.wordpress.com.

Stephen Sottong

Stephen Sottong lives in beautiful northern California behind the Redwood Curtain. He writes Science Fiction, Fantasy and Mystery. A full list of publications is at stephensottong.com.

Ryan Tan

Ryan Tan lives in Singapore. His fiction is forthcoming in *The Halloween Book* and *The 13 Days of Christmas*. He is currently studying English Literature at the National University of Singapore.

Darren Todd

Darren Todd's work has been published in more than thirty publications over the last fifteen years, most recently in Breaking Rules Publishing's anthology, *The Hollow Vol 3*, Puppycat Press's *Invoking Chaos*, and Sley House Publishing's *Tales of the Sley House, 2021*. In 2022, he has a story appearing in a Chilling Tales for Dark Nights print anthology and one for their Tiny Terrors podcasts.

Chad A.B. Wilson

Chad A.B. Wilson's work has been previously published in *Savage Realms Monthly*, *HyphenPunk*, *SFS Stories*, and *Swords and Sorcery Magazine*, and will be published in the upcoming anthologies *Dragons and Heroines*, *Road Kill: Texas Horror by Texas Writers*, and *Slaughter is the Best Medicine*.

Jasiah Witkofsky

The anti-villain known as Jasiah Witkofsky is an independent author, editor, philosopher-gardener, artistic dabbler, rock n' roller, and rabblerouser dwelling amidst the majestic Sierra Nevadas of Northern California. His works can be found on both hemispheres of the globe, three continents, from several anthology companies.

Find him on Facebook: @jasiahwitkofskyauthorpage

Gray W. Wolfe

Gray W. Wolfe is a published author of nine short stories in several anthologies with Dragon Soul Press, Black Ink Fiction, and Carpathian Publishing. His motto is:

Blood. Tears. Carnage.

Grim Fantasy

Prey Welcome

J.D. Wolff

J.D. Wolff is sometimes a biologist, sometimes a writer, but mostly a reader. She loves fiction.

Sheldon Woodbury

Sheldon Woodbury has an MFA in Dramatic Writing from New York University where he also taught screenwriting. He's an award-winning writer (screenplays, plays, books, short stories, and poems). His book *Cool Million* is considered the essential guide to writing high concept movies. His short stories and poems have appeared in many horror anthologies and magazines. His novel, *The World on Fire*, was published in September, 2014, by JWK Fiction. His poem, "The Midnight Circus," was selected by Ellen Datlow as an honourable mention for *Best Horror 2017*, and his poem, "The Madness of Monsters," is included in the 2021 *HWA Poetry Showcase*.

ABOUT THE PUBLISHER

BLACK HARE PRESS is a small, independent publisher based in Melbourne, Australia.

Founded in 2018, our aim has always been to champion emerging authors from all around the globe and offer opportunities for them to participate in speculative fiction and horror short story anthologies.

Connect

Website: www.blackharepress.com
Twitter: @BlackHarePress

ACKNOWLEDGEMENTS

When we embarked on our Black Hare Press journey back in late 2018, we never envisioned the huge support we'd get from the writing community. We have been truly humbled by the number of submissions we've received.

So, thank you to everyone who crafted tales just for us—we thank you from the bottom of our hearts. To our families and friends, collaborators, random strangers who took pity on us, and everyone who has helped us on the way: we couldn't have done it without you. Special thanks to our Patreon supporters, especially S. Jade Path, James Aitchison, and Jonathan Stiffy. Take a look at the Patreon-only content and merch here—patreon.com/blackharepress—and consider helping us get to the next stage.

And to you, our discerning reader, we and these talented writers did it all for you. We hope you enjoyed these tales, and if you did, don't forget to leave a review.

Love & kisses, The Team

Made in the USA
Middletown, DE
31 July 2023